This book is the first in a series of books written by Deborah Crossley Hatswell which feature witness reports collected over 40 years. Deborah uses the word 'paranormal' in its widest sense to describe the creatures that are being seen. Paranormal simply means 'around normal' or just 'on the edge of normal' and as these Creatures are beyond our understanding, and are still in the realm of theory there is no real word or genre that can describe them. Impossible Creatures and Unexplained events happen to ordinary people in towns and cities worldwide every day. In this book you will hear from the witnesses themselves as they take you back to the day of the event. You will read of encounters with Ape Men, Dog men, Unseen predators and Hairy Bipedal creatures.

I would of course like to thank every witness who reached out to me over the decades and shared their own experiences, I know just how hard it can be to not only find someone to report your encounter too but the very idea of speaking it out loud to another human can be paralysing for some, myself included. Thank you for trusting me enough in the beginning to open up, and for our many conversations over the years as together we thrash around theory and thought in the hopes of one day working all this out, what we saw and experienced in a world that does not accept anything "out of the box" or "alternative" in any way.

And for the people out there who may one day be a future witness to something similar, remember you are not alone, in fact we are many. All of the accounts contained in the book came into me personally or were resourced on the internet by myself and the research team.

I would also like to thank my family who have helped me every step of the way, My Daughters, Husband and Grandchildren. Who each have their own path to walk, whilst also helping me to walk mine. I wish them love, happiness and strength in all things.

To my Mum and my late Father who taught me to stand up for myself always, regardless of Foe. T. J. Crossley 46 - 18 I send you my love always.

People Who Witness 'Paranormal' Creatures - How many times have you heard the statement *"I would love to see something like that"* or *"wow your so lucky, I would give anything to see one up close"* Or my favourite *"why didn't you take a picture to prove what you saw"* Being a witness to something impossible is not the lovely spiritual meeting most imagine. In this book I will explain what it is really like being a child witness to something nobody could explain away or smooth over quickly, or a hurried explanation given by a parent who wants to help their child but doesn't know how to.

 Children have vivid imaginations or flights of fancy and it's something we encourage in them, but that can be a double edged sword, it was for me and in writing this book I'm hoping I can express how it feels to spend your whole life trying to prove to others that you are in fact not mad or in need of medical intervention. You simply saw something one day that has an effect on your entire life.

As children we don't ask to see "them" or set out equipped like a researcher hoping for a glimpse of said creature or monster, it happens by happenstance, a fleeting moment frozen in time, that face etched in your memory and for most of us it was a horrifying traumatic experience that refuses to go away. The fear contained within these encounters can leave some witnesses with an almost PTSD condition affecting them through life, and although the fear may lessen as we look at it with adult eyes, it never really leaves.

To be honest, deep down we will always be that child frozen in those seconds of time. I struggled for decades with my encounter and I know many of the witnesses in this book did the same. Hopefully we have now set in place somewhere people can report these events too and receive validation that we are not alone, as I show each witnesses a validation account in the same area they encountered their "creature" or where the "monsters" description fits with what they saw too, it gives the person involved a feeling of "companionship" a feeling of being believed by others who understand. Sometimes these validation reports can take decades to be reported, or are future sightings that have not yet taken place.

But each new report fits like a cog into this huge puzzle we have, sometimes that cog enables a door to open or a screen to slide and we suddenly understand a small pattern of behaviour or a match in description or habitat. In this book you will notice the term "green belt" mentioned in most of the accounts, there does seem to be a pattern to all of these experiences regardless of what County the event took place. Children playing on disused land, old crofts and scrubland, building swings and playing in the woods along these routes.

If I could start my research career from this point rather than 30 something years ago, I would probably have used the term "Green Belt Creatures" the words are used so often. The witnesses I encounter are not only children, they are aged between 6 - 83, from all walks of life, sensible people doing everyday tasks who see something impossible to explain. Many of the adult accounts start with "I was out with the dog" or "I was just taking my usual walk" but that's for another book and another time, and I need to take you back to 1982 when everything changed for me and the world has never been the same since.

I grew up in an ordinary town, my Mum worked for the Local Authority and my Dad worked at the famous Boddingtons Brewery, my Family have worked the Docks and Mines of Salford for generations. My Grandfather owned the local scrap yard or (tatters) as they were called then, a Man with a horse and cart who collected any metal you didn't want or any junk that was of no use and he would reward you with a "dolly blu" a "donkey stone" or a balloon in return.

Simple hardworking folk who lived in this very ordinary mill town in the North West of England. Salford is a working class town, bombed heavily in the second World War due to the Manchester Ship Canal that runs through our town, the River Irwell rolls down from the North and out to sea and the Valley it rolls along was my playground as a child, back then there were limited restrictions on fun, riding the cart horses or catching sticklebacks in jam jars and frogspawn carried home in your welly. We would build wooden "dens" that were guarded by fierce children with stones and "duckers" at the ready to defend these forts. Ideal times and fond memories.

As a child of the town I was very lucky in the sense that my family would take off for weekends and school holidays to the countryside or the beach, my Grandfather Ged would take us to the horse fairs and fetes where hundreds of families from the towns and countryside would meet,sell livestock and share tall tales. My Grandad had Horses and Ducks, Geese and Chickens, we raised Jack Russell Terriers and my Dad raised some of the best Greyhounds to come out of Ireland in the 80's and 90's and we travelled to race them at every Dog track across the North West, my Dad was also an avid fisherman and my Sisters and I grew up on the banks of the Rivers that flow here.

The Severn and the Trent have some of my most treasured memories growing up, getting up at 4am to load the car or van, lunches packed and flasks filled, bait and rods and kids in the back, every trip a different woodland or copse. But in 1982 all that stopped for me, the places I used to play had another connotation that year, where I had never experienced fear there was now a hidden danger in every bush, an enemy behind every tree, hidden down in every ditch.

It was an ordinary day, those perfect days between Spring and Summer when it's not too hot and the breeze blows easily with no hint of rain or a cloud in the sky. Days when school seemed like a punishment and School Jumpers were compulsory and thousands of hot tired teenagers would be taking their "mock" exams heads nodding and sweat building, myself included. The school I attended was an old victorian mansion owned by the SummerHill family, the grounds that surrounded it were nice but a little left to the wild, the park was directly across from the school, the new school building was added a few decades before and was a square concrete assault on the eyes with a thousand windows or so it seemed, really easy for a teacher to spy you skipping school, or school kid wishing they had also skipped would point out the window and dob you in.

I had skipped the odd day before (Mum if you're reading this it's too late to ground me) I found the academic side of school easy and I would get bored so quickly, most of my days spent staring out the window daydreaming,the social side was a complete puzzle to me and I just winged it most days hoping I had used the correct response or had not shouted out inappropriately when I found something exciting or it held my interest. I had a lot of friends back then, all in a similar position no doubt, you just don't realise as a child most of your friends have the same fears and peer pressure. So I was never one to say no to a new adventure. I did have one particular friend back then I spent most of my time with, my partner in crime so to speak, much braver than I and usually to be found smoking round the back of the gym or in smokers corner as we called it.

I had gone into my lessons in the morning and had only two study periods after lunch, so I wasn't missing anything other than revision and it was too nice of a day to be stuck indoors.

Lunch would be two sittings between 12 noon and 1.30 pm I can't remember what sitting I was on that week but I remember being in 4 year and we had a rotation because the walk between the two buildings could take 15 minutes and we could do that walk 4 times a day. I don't remember much "before I saw "him" or for about an hour and a half (the time it took me to get home) after the event.

Theres is an old Edwardian House in the middle of the park, country gardens, golf course and meadow, animal enclosures with goats, Rabbits, Horses and a menagerie of birds, there was a fantastic "glass house" with tropical plants from all across the world, like a huge rain forest within a glass dome. The "glass house" was always hot, steam would rise from the huge Koi pond in the centre, there was also a screened Butterfly house which was like a steamy bath, most folks called it the "hot house."

The "hot house" was open to the public and could be visited for free, there was also a sensory garden for the blind. Lots of tactile and heavily scented plants and herbs with Braille metal plaques beneath each flower or shrub. Everytime I smell Lavender or Wild Garlic I'm transported right back to warm childhood days. The gardens in the 70's were beautifully tended, one of my family members worked there and My Dad would take me everytime he had the chance. I have many pictures of myself as a kid in Buile Hill until that day in 82.

By 1982, the park was in a rougher state, many of the groundsmen had been laid off, the old house was in the process of being turned into an Art Gallery or a mining museum, it has changed so many times over the decades and now stands broken, deserted and vandalised. It's a very sorry sight indeed.

Between the House and the Sensory garden was an old Victorian flower bed, which sound delightful but it was a tangle of weeds by this point, Laurel and Box Privet all intertwined with the Rhododendrons and Ivy left to grow to around 25 ft high and in between all of that was flattened down area almost like a bed of some kind and we would climb in through the brambles and nettles and from your position in there you could see out, but people passing by would have no idea you were in there at all. So if you stayed quiet and kept yourself hidden in there till around 3.20 pm you could walk home with the other kids and it looked like you had been to school all along. That was the plan for the afternoon and then within two hours I was running from that Park, crying and screaming running from a monster I thought had come to kill me and he was probably in hot pursuit in my mind, without thinking I ran home without any real thought given to the action.

My only fear that day was being caught "wagging" it, it wouldn't have been fun being marched in school the day after, with a clipped ear as a reminder by my Mother who wouldn't stand for much messing about on my part. Or some older kids who would move us off and into the open where the odd teacher sneaking a quick smoke would see us or one of the "parkies" who would drag you back to school sharpish given the chance. I remember talking about "top of the pops" and the charts and I think we were making plans for what to do that evening after tea, we were laughing and giggling and sat in a sprawled position on the grass just looking up at the sky and forgetting we were running the risk of being caught, we forgot to be quiet and to be honest were making a racket as most teenage girls do.

I remember looking up and watching the leaves as they moved and out of the corner of my eye in my peripheral vision I saw for a split second a movement in the shade, I looked at it thinking "bird" or "cat" but nothing moved at all, like that moment before the storm hits, or the ship runs aground, when everything goes quiet as your brain processes the danger your in, and sends that signal to your legs to run, I realised what I was looking at was not the colour of a bird or the flash of a ginger tom, but eyes, eyes the same colour as amber contained in an impossible face. Even in that moment being a down to earth girl I thought "oh god it's a teacher, we are in for it now" excuses already being chosen in my head, if only I had thought to run then, before he looked out, before I saw a face I can never forget, no matter how hard I tried to.

Before I could raise from the ground, before my legs started to run, before I screamed a scream I have never duplicated in my 51 years, I saw something that looked like a man and an ape had been combined in some way, pushed together to form one unit. Hairy with hair that was long and dark, the darkest brown, with highlights of auburn as the sun caught it, which in a way sounds romantic, but it wasn't, it was like the colour of a red setter before it bites the hand holding the biscuit, something so beautiful in colour but yet deadly and smarts long after the injury.

That sentence *"he looked like a man and an ape combined"* is one I have used to describe him ever since, simply because that's what he looked like, an old caveman weathered and worn, or an escaped ape that was somehow human at the same time. A Neanderthal or Troglodyte looking creature with hair everywhere, he had a thick jaw and a pronounced brow ridge, a terrifying face with a slack jaw looking back at me from within that mess of foliage. I don't remember a smell, or a sound, just terror, I looked at him then at my friend, and without even knowing why as we we rose to run I pushed her hard, as hard as I could to the ground without even thinking through the process, now I know it was primal instinct to survive. I have felt guilty about that moment every time I think of it, even now. I was up and running and as I looked behind me to see A. if he was in pursuit or B. that she was up and running too, I saw him simply melt back into the greenery as if he was never there to start with.

He had teeth like ours, not fanged or pointed like a dog, square like a human just larger, at a guess and from my position he was taller than a tall man, probably around 7 ft in height, with dark tanned skin and even though he had a weathered face I don't think he was old, more that he lived outside in the sun, like the men who used to tarmac the road, darkly tanned and weathered. His eyes were like ours but not clean and white, more a yellowed or a jaundiced look to them, I concentrated on his eyes and his teeth, waiting for him to rush out and grab us and begin to do whatever he did with teenage girls he found in the woods, or an arm to hit me with such force I would be flat on my back and easy prey within seconds. But none of that happened, she ran one way towards Salford Precinct and I ran like the wind till I made it home, being physically sick a number of times on the run, running every green space through my head till I got in.

I didn't care about punishment, I didn't care how mad she was going to be, I ran in the door expecting my Mum to drop to her knees and comfort me, to receive the reply "bloody hell Deb, what've done to your uniform it's a right mess" was not the reaction I needed. She whipped my jumper off and pushed me to the kitchen sink, all the while I'm trying to explain about the Ape man that had tried to get me while my Mums saying "don't be silly it was probably just a tramp, don't tell your Dad you didn't go in school or you will be in for it" at which point I burst into tears all over again and tried to explain over and over what had happened. At first her answered made me really upset and I couldn't stop the tears, then I got mad, mad at not being believed and a little bit mad that they had not warned me about things like this, if there is a crazy Ape like thing out there, surely adults would know and warn you off, then came the realisation that Mum wasn't brushing me off just because she had her hands full with my Dad, me and my sister to see too, two jobs and an ageing parent to care for and was just "done" with my drama, it was she did not have a clue, and that meant neither did anyone else. The realisation I was on my own with this one was the most awful feeling I have ever felt.

Years later in my 30's as a single Mum of two I was told "you will probably never walk unaided again" after a really bad accident, and that shook me to the core, but it was nothing compared to that cold sickly feeling in the very pit of your stomach when a fear becomes a reality. When your whole world suddenly becomes blurry and you feel like your knees will give way as the sudden realisation that you have to go back there tomorrow and for another 6 months or so until you leave to start college. I don't think I slept a wink for weeks,every shadow was him or his kind, every noise or bang, sudden running footsteps were no longer just another kid running, but one of "his" kind coming for you.

That fear stayed with me,through my teens and my 20's never mentioned out loud like the massive Ape man in the room, or if mentioned brushed of with "oh your so dramatic, it was just a homeless man" "are you still going on about that, you would think at this age, you would be over that by now" So I stopped talking about it, stopped saying how confused and scared I was, I buckled everything down and went off the rails for a good few years there.

Marriage and children didn't quell it, no holidays in the woods or camping trips, I remember a work colleague offered me her centre parks cabin in the woods for free for two weeks and the horror in my face at the idea gave her the impression I was an incredibly ungrateful friend who should probably count her blessings as she stormed off in a huff, but I was just stood there flummoxed not knowing what to say or how I could explain my actions without actually having to tell her why. The amount of times my parents went off for holidays and weekends and I would stay behind with my Nan safe in a tall block of flats away from "him and his kind."

Don't get me wrong I have walked the streets of Salford as most of us have growing up at night in the dark, it's a terraced house, cobbled streets, car lights, people everywhere type of town. Like most people with "phobias" I learnt to hide it, to adapt my world around it so it didn't seem like a problem anymore and somehow I managed to file it away for long periods of time but deep down it was always there in the background, chipping away until I realised that I had to find others who may have seen him too which would make "him" a reality, or my best hope others who may know about something that could explain all this away, a local circus visit maybe, or some ape film being made? Here I am 37 yrs later writing it down for others to read, I did find them, and they were not hard to find, people like me, hundreds of them with stories like mine, and here in this book you will hear their stories too.

37yrs on from my encounter I have collected over 500 reports in the UK and in the last 2yrs those sighting reports have spread across Europe and Asia, America and Russia each week another report comes in which of course is another witness out there feeling alone. I would like to share all of these accounts with you from every corner of the world, but first let's concentrate on the child witnesses as this is where my journey began, and I hope as your read these pages settled with a cuppa on the sofa or on a warm day relaxing in the garden pondering life, give thought to all the other children out there who never got to report what happened, and what thoughts and feelings they are left with.

As an adult, one of the hardest things we do is to put our head up above the parapet and speak out loudly knowing all around you heads will shake, eyes will roll and you will be met with utter disbelief. Adults have coping skills, cognitive minds that reason, as a child you have nothing like this, the grown ups own all the answers. Back then I had no real sense of self, nothing to reason what "he" was and any stray wisp of "self" left within you will be wiped out in the weeks to come with the constant explaining of how *"you didn't see it"* or "it was a homeless man" or my absolute favourite *"she's always been a bit dramatic"* and I admit that on occasion I was prone to childish exaggeration and flights of imagination as all children are.

What happened to me that day back in 1982 changed my whole life forever, and left me with more fears than any child should have, more questions than leaves on a tree, left to work it all out on my own the "monster" each child saw grows in size and ability, arms although of the large variety, in your head become arms that can stretch around the corner and grab you as you run up the stairs to the flat as fast as you can, arms that will reach from under every bush and hedge, every tree a blind for him to hide behind and every shadow becomes a 7ft Apeman that surely wants to eat you and will come looking for you in the night. His height grows each year in your head, so woodland visits and night camping become things you did "before" and your life is sectioned in two, before the incident and after. Never explaining just accepting there are things you loved you can no longer do, memories no longer made, just nagging doubts, hours of searching online and a need for a place to report this too, to find other like you who are out there alone with just the questions we all have rolling around in our heads.

You don't know at 15 you will one day help others in your situation, help them to bring their stories forward, help them to stand up and say "me too, I saw it and nobody ever believed me" words we have all said, all of us who see the "wild ones" the "hair covered ones" the creature people now refer to as the British Bigfoot but who back then was the Apeman and somewhere deep inside he still is that to me.

No matter how many people I help, whether male or female we all have a shared experience, a trauma left within us and nowhere to go. And I hope writing this book will give you an idea of just what it is like to be one of the unfortunate fortunate ones!

I normally get three reactions when I share my story, the classic eye roll and cuckoo noises happen the most, then the well known friend of a friend's story, but on more occasions than you will believe I see a spark of recognition, a cog turns and a story starts to unravel, remembered from childhood of things pushed way down within, as looking at them would make it all real and you will be right back there in your head, right back to the time you dread to think of, because it makes you remember that you have seen things that make you question the very core of man and this world we think we know so well.

Am I the only one who has seen this? I asked myself over and over, do they not know these things live out there? or worse do the adults know and just choose to ignore it?

Back then I didn't know which one was the scariest option, they all weighed the same to me. I knew that all the tales that we were told of humans being the only thing that walks the planet on human legs and feet, well other than the Great Apes of course were wrong. Sadly what we witnessed was not Human or Ape, it was a blend of the two somehow? And it would take decades for each of us to find each other, to find people prepared to help, prepared to hear us out, without judgement.

Like any person who has an experience with Alien life, or someone who saw a ghost, we just ask that you hear us out, listen to what we have to say about the things we saw as children, maybe you too have witnessed something similar or you may hold a tiny piece of the puzzle that helps each witness to understand their experience within your hand all the time without realising.

For the sake of ease I will call each creature witnessed a "British Bigfoot" that's the trendy name, the name fashion brings, for me he is the Woodwose, our Man in the woods, the Greenman of old, Herne or Pan even, that's after 35 yrs of researching the theory I have settled on. So I started searching in dusty book shops and newspaper archives. MSN and CB radio were a good source for me in the early days, contacting truckers and drivers here and in as many countries as I could find, asking if they too had seen anything, joining camping groups and woodland walkers in the hopes one of the people included would hear me out or have a tale of their own to tell. And the emergence of the wonderful world wide web gave me another tool to search with and I was lucky enough to contact many American and Canadian witnesses, Russians and Europeans also. Some of the old names in Bigfoot were really happy to share encounters or research tips.

Plugging away on my own for years was hard but it did enable me to build a knowledge base of the Sasquatch people that live across the world. The images and descriptions they shared fitted, they looked like the figure I saw, mine a slightly smaller version, like the Russian Almasty or the Leshy and Puka's of old, A hair covered "man" with an ape like face, naked, no clothing is ever reported. Large hands and feet are seen not paws or hooves.

Wild humans is how I think of them but there are a whole host of theories behind "what they are" "where they come from"? I strongly feel that it is for each witness to choose the theory that works for them, in this book I would just like to bring you their stories as they happened. In their own words as they speak of their experiences, what changed for them afterwards and what happened to them on the day in question.

I have included some Adult witness accounts as they are in the immediate area or have the same MO so to speak. I call these validation accounts, not all of the witnesses get validation and It is one of the things we strive for. I hope reading the accounts contained in the book will give not only validation but a few more people may just feel that the time is right to tell their story.

Other Witnesses to the Salford Ape Man - Little did I know back then in 1982 I was not the first person to encounter a strange hairy naked man in the park in my hometown, much earlier in 1974 a gentleman had already made a report of a *"small hairy naked man who was chasing a fox."* It was many decades later in Jan 2019 when I was contacted by a Gentleman from the area who like myself has family links that go back generations and had a very similar upbringing to myself, many would call him a down to earth working class man with nothing to gain by sharing with me a story he had heard so many times before told to him by his family members.

A Little Hairy Man Chasing a Fox. 1970's - Witness Report. PV: *There is a story in my family that I have heard since I was a lad, One told to me by my family member who had finished work one night who was waiting in the Park area waiting for his work mate to arrive for his lift home. He was waiting on the corner of Eccles Old Road and as he had been in transit all day had not had a chance to answer a pressing need and was caught short whilst waiting, he went on to explain that after looking around for somewhere private he remembered there were a couple of public toilet blocks in Buile Hill Park and the ones next to the old Mansion were the nearest.*

So he nipped into the park for a quick call of nature, The toilets were locked tight after 4pm, so he had to use the overgrown bushes alongside them and as he did so something caught his eye, he looked a little closer and said to his surprise he saw a strange "short hairy man, that was trying to catch a fox" It startled him a little so he made off pretty quickly and has only really ever shared this with family members to this day. I think he would be very pleased to know he was not the only person to see something strange in that Park. I know that area really well and it is in fact a number of parks that line the route, Seedley Park, Buile Hill Park and Light Oaks Park all have ample hiding spaces and enough squirrel to feed an army, a short walk to the Irwell River Valley and from there you access any area you want in all four directions".

Witness Report: Brenda 84 - This account was sent to Thomas Marcum of the Crypto Crew, When he heard me speaking about my sighting and where it happened he sent the account over to me.

"I recently read your article with a lady named Deborah, who saw the Yeti Bigfoot in Buile Hill park in Salford and I wanted to get in touch because I saw the same thing in 1984 when I was 30 years old. I was walking my dog there as I did often and it was a freezing cold day and I was having a cigarette and trying to keep warm until the dog had finished his walk. It was dark at that time of year at 5pm and I thought I was alone in the park as it is usually shut up by then but this particular night it was open. (the park has a number of entrances and some would be locked whilst others remained open all night) I was just standing smoking when a movement to my left caught my eye.

There was nearby light just beyond the toilet block and I saw this tall "thing" just standing there. It looked to me to be about 6 foot tall and was quite podgy. "It" had a bit of a rounded belly on "It" What got me right away was that it had bare feet, it was freezing outside and "thing" was standing there with nothing covering "Its" feet. It was then that I noticed "It" also was completely nude, "It" had no clothing on at all but it had hair all over the body.

That's when I thought it must have been someone playing silly beggars with me but this "thing" just stood there. I clearly saw "It" had male genitalia and that was when I became worried, I realised I was a lone female on my own with this thing in an empty dark at dusk. I thought "It" might attack me. "It" just stood there staring for about 20 seconds and then "It" turned very quickly and ran off into the trees. I quickly left the park and returned home and told my then boyfriend and his brother but he laughed and said I must have seen the local perv trying to pick up a prostitute.

I will never forget that thing. I did not know anything about Bigfoot and stuff but that's what it must have been, and to learn someone else saw it in the same trees was startling. I would never forget it. It looked like a chimp but with the body shape of a man. It couldn't have been a monkey because it was too tall and it was like a caveman from the dinosaur days. It had a piggy type of nose and large black eyes. It was full of brown hair and it had a human's face but it was also like a chimps. It is hard to explain. I would like my email kept secret from the public as I don't want hate mail but thought I would get in touch because that lady saw the same thing in the park as me. It is not easy talking about these things in an ordinary town like Salford, I was worried they would look me up and throw the key away to be honest".

As you see, validation did eventually happen for me, and there are a number of accounts all along the River Irwell Route some of which are within this book, there are also a number of stories yet to be shared that I have found in my home town and a number of towns that border it. And I will of course be writing about those two, but for now I would like to concentrate on the child witnesses and some of the accounts that brought them validation and a feeling of being believed and accepted.

I was contacted by a lovely lady named Karen who had an experience many years ago in childhood that has stayed with her throughout her life, trying to find answers to explain what she saw or how it was even possible this experience had happened to her she searched online and found others who had experienced the very same things. A strange man- like creature that others claimed to her was impossible, but like myself Karen and many others saw that impossible "creature" was so real it is still with us to this day, decades later the old questions of "how" "who" and "what" and "why me" never go away. Hopefully by sharing her story with others Karen can finally find some answers and hopefully find others who have had the same experience and are out there thinking they too are alone.

A Witness to a Wild Man. Stanley, 1974 - Witness Report. Karen: *"I'm hoping you can help me as I had a strange experience as a child that I'd like to share. I'm hoping to shed some light on what happened to me that day and some help in working out what "he" was. I was somewhere between 5-7 years old and I was in the local woods in Stanley co. Durham I was with some older children just playing out as children do. There was a group of us playing in the woods and climbing trees and making all kinds of noise. The girls I was with were about 13 years old and nice sensible girls so my parents allowed me to tag along with them whenever I got the chance.*

Where I lived back then was an ordinary house in an ordinary town in the North East of England. There were lots of fields and woods to explore, but it wasn't remote or dense in any sense of the world. It was an average town really with surrounding countryside and green belt land, lots of small woods and streams scattered about.

From what I can remember we were playing in a clearing and I think there may have been a rope swing attached to the tree, we were all playing and for some reason I looked up into a tree, and high in the branches I could see a really strange 'Man' he was crouched down and he was holding a knife in one of his hands. He wasn't like a normal man who was just out of place, not a tramp or a boy playing tricks, of course all this I reasoned afterwards. The "Man" I was looking up at I called an Ape Man or a Monkey Man as there are no other words to describe him. He reminded me of a caveman or Wildman who had lived out in the wilds his whole life. I have included a picture I found online that resembles what I saw that day.

I can't remember a lot of details about his appearance after 30 yrs or so. He had long bushy dark hair and wore no clothes at all. In panic I pointed him out to the girls that were with me and they looked up but they said no one was there? I ran from the woods crying in fear with the girls chasing after me trying to catch up to me and calm me down. They always insisted that no one was there, which you think would explain the whole thing away but the fact only I could see him in a way was worse, I was hoping they would say it was just someone dressed up or playing a prank to explain why he was there but they never did.

That really worried me over the years and on occasion you question yourself harder than any skeptic. Constantly trying to explain all this away, hoping all of a sudden some tiny thought *would give way to "ahh now I understand" but that never came. And even to this day my Husband and Family buy me monkey gifts or toys, I have never hidden this from anyone, this experience is part of me, part of my story, and one of the reasons I'm myself, it is my story, of a terrifying sighting of a hairy man, who looked like a monkey with a knife gripped tightly in his hand.*

I could see him just as clearly as he could see me. He wasn't like a Bigfoot or what I'd imagine they would look like, but he wasn't like a normal human man either. I know for sure I definitely saw him that day and it frightened me to think the girls I was with couldn't see him and that there is no explanation of who or what he was".

Little did we know another reader in the same BBR Facebook group saw Karen's post and got in touch with us as he too had an encounter in the very same town, many years later. He went on to describe a certain part of the coast to coast road that always gave him the feeling he was being watched. And even though he had cycled this way on many an occasion, one night stands out to him above all others.

Hiding In The Church Yard. Stanley, 2006 - Witness Report. D. L: *"Hi Deborah, Can you put me in touch with a lady who contacted you because she had an encounter with an Apeman/Wildman in the Stanley County Durham area. I was hoping to chat with you as I don't live too far away from the location that she had the encounter in and there is another location along that same road where I used to ride my bicycle between my girlfriends house and where I used to live back then. It was on one certain part of the road that I always felt like I was being watched by something, it felt like something I couldn't see was watching me from the shadows and I knew something was there but could never see anything.*

As it would often be late at night when I would be returning home it was usually pretty dark and on one occasion I saw something big standing behind a large tree near a graveyard and church. I believe whatever "It" was "It" had followed me as I rode along the whole of my journey until I got to the main road and the feeling was gone? I didn't have the feeling I was being watched as long as I was on the main part of the road to my house.

This particular night I was on the way to my girlfriends, so it would have been around 8pm. We both lived in Co Durham but in different towns so as I said I rode this route a lot. I used to cycle to my girlfriends house and she lived in the Harelaw Stanley area. I would bike it from my house in Consett. The area itself is on the Coast to Coast path in between Consett and Stanley. It's mostly fields or woods along the main road and it runs alongside farmland with a few dense patches of woodland.

At the Consett side of that route is a church with a graveyard and a dense row of trees at the other side of the path behind the church, as soon as I got onto that path I got the feeling that I was being watched again, so I looked around everywhere, I couldn't see anything so I just continued on with my journey.

When I was on my way home it took me about 10 to 15 minutes to get to the church and I heard a noise behind the trees where I had felt something was watching me from. So I slowed down to get a good look, my eyes adjusted and I saw a Large Dark Figure standing behind a tree that was roughly about 7 to 71/2 feet tall. I couldn't make out any facial features or fine detail as it was dark and the only light I had to see by was on the front of my bike.

I didn't want to stick around and had no thoughts of approaching it to see what it was or to get a closer look so I quickly left. Now it would usually take about 10 minutes to get to the end of that path and that night I did it in about 4 minutes.

This area has a lot of open land and trees, and close to the end of one section there is an area that has about 6 short hairpin type turns, with 10 foot high embankments on either side that these turns go around and there big and go deep enough back that something or someone could hide in and not be seen until it was too late. My encounter was on the coast to coast route between consett county durham and stanley County Durham".

Whenever a sighting comes in I make a note of it by adding it to a map of accounts I have made over the decades, this map enables me to see not only if there are other creature reports in the area but also any reports of howls, growls, shadowing footsteps that keep in step with you and also any reports where dogs and animals react out of character also. It gives me and my readers an idea of what is moving around where and what possible activity we can connect to the accounts. This is one account close to Stanley that shows something that can scare a dog is hiding in those woods.

The Dene Dog Alert, Wood Knocks, North East. January 2018 - Witness Report: *"I just thought I would tell you of an incident that happened while I was out walking with my dog last week. I tend to walk the same route every night and a part of this route is through woodland, we walk there as it is a nice area to walk and there is a path following along by a stream.*

The terrain on either side of the stream banks and rises steeply on both sides, on one side leads to a road and on the other leads to open fields. My Westie dog is 6 1/2 years old and has walked these paths for nearly all her life without any problems at all. However, on this particular night, as we approached the Dene she started to stay very close to me, so close that at times I nearly tripped over her. This is not her usual demeanor at all. And that's why I started to take note of her behaviour.

She kept doing this, which is very unlike her and I didnt know what to think. So I just kept trying to get her to walk the way we usually went, I kept trying to steer her that way. When we got to the Dene entrance, which is an old car park that is no longer accessible to cars, she flatly refused to go any further. The dog would not move?

She was pulling back and trying to go back the way we had come and when I got a hold of her and managed to get her closer to me she cowered and growled, I think she was really scared of something I couldn't see? In the end I had to give up and turn back the way we had come. As we left the area and crossed the main road I heard what I would describe as a very loud, sharp wood knock. Only the one knock and apart from the area being unusually quiet there was nothing else out of the ordinary.

I have walked through the Dene every night since and have had no further strange incidents and my dog has carried on as she did before, as if the events of that night never happened? This was a strange occurrence in my experience, I am in my 60's now and have been an outdoor sort of person all my life, shooting, camping, hiking and dog walking which I have done at all times of the day and night without any kind of fear or an incident like this, When I *was working shifts I often walked my dogs after midnight and thought nothing of walking through the fields and woods where I live. I still do but now there is a nagging little doubt, Is there something out there?*

I am unaware if there are any sightings in my area, I do know of a sighting of a large cat type of animal on the prowl, so it could be that's what scared her? The odd sheep goes missing now and again which we have put down to rustlers, perhaps we are wrong about that. This has affected me somewhat, not to the point where I won't go out but now when I hear things like Pheasants flying off in alarm, sheep being alarmed etc. there is another question to answer".

I did advise the witness that there are a number of accounts of dogs being spooked, refusing to move, and in some cases, running off and leaving the owner or person behind in a desperate bid to get away. As a dog owner myself I have learnt to trust my dogs when out, a loud barking is the dogs way of scaring something off, if they become very quiet and on occasion protect their midriff then the threat is perceived as being "too large to handle alone."

I don't think it was the area itself that caused the dog to behave in this way, more something she sensed that we humans did not pick up on. I decided to see just how many accounts are on the UK sightings map, and there are a lot of accounts where the dog alarmed first and refused to enter an area. I think my favourite account is the account from Yorkshire where the gentleman out walking his dog River was confronted with a 7ft hairy man who walked out of the wood line and looked quickly to the left as if to warn "others" in the tree line, the gentleman in question was so startled he promptly nodded in acknowledgement and said "alreet" to the creature then hurried went back the way he had come.

A **Rope Swing Nightmare** - Witness Report. Shaine Winfrow: *"When I was 14 years old, I was out in the woods close to my home in a place we went to all the time, It was a wooded area with streams and rope swings and we played there a lot doing the usual boy's games, building forts and ramps for bikes, obstacle courses where we would play and make lots of noise whilst just having fun with your mates. On that day I had gone into the woods with my brother and another of our friends. We were messing about as usual for a while and then we decided we would make a better rope swing. It didn't take long to make the rope swing and start playing on It.*

I should say we were in Cat woods in Sheffield. I have always called it this but it doesn't show up on maps under any name? It must just be a local name, I think. Anyway we were swinging and making a racket but over the top of that we could hear something or someone moving about in the bushes and shrub and it sounded like some kind of animal coming close to where we were. At this point we couldn't see it but you heard it clearly, and whatever "It" was "It" was making a howling snarling noise as it was getting closer. And closer to us. At the time I thought we had disturbed a dog or some wild animal or it was some of our mates playing a prank and at any moment they would jump out and say "got you."

We were looking around everywhere to try and see what it was making the noises. It was at this point that we looked up into the tree canopy where the rope swing was tied to a branch, but much further up in the tree branches above our heads we saw something unexplainable standing on the branches further up in the tree, it was black and grey and stood on two feet, one foot placed on each branch, My head was on a swivel looking up and down trying to work out what it was and that is when I realised there was also a "one of them" but smaller across from us just watching us.

The small one was the size of a small child. We realised we were between the younger "one" and the adult "one" standing above us, so as you can imagine we ran so fast out of there and didn't stop running until we were a good distance away. We spent most of the evening trying to explain all this away as a trick or prank and we decided the only way to make any sense of this was to go back in there and look, it wasn't something I wanted to do, but I didn't want to look like a wimp in front of my brother and my friend so I knew I would have to do it.

We went back a day later to get the rope swing as we thought the rope swing had something to do with the encounter and somehow removing it would make all this go away, but it was ripped apart in pieces and the ground around it was covered in black and grey hair and that was so unnerving we never went back there again.

That day has never left me and I have spent the years in between collecting accounts from other people in the area and going as far back in newspaper articles as I could looking for others, I joined camping groups and any outdoor online forums, anywhere I could think of to be honest, just trying to work out what "they" were. Today if I had to explain it I would describe them as "Bigfoot type creatures" , hair covered and Ape like, almost like a man and a monkey at the same time. I have searched the area too, I have *found sewer pipes and tunnels underground and I have found lots of local accounts of "dark walking figures" and one person who reported howls. Less than 4 miles away in another small wood there is an almost identical account at Hackenthorpe, you can move quite easily between the two woods at dusk or dawn quite easily".*

I have spoken with this witness over the years and I asked him what the "creature" by the stream looked like in more detail, he went on to say "it looked like a heavy set chimp, and it stood like chimps do with it's knuckles on the ground and it was kind of swaying a little bit as if it was agitated." Now that I'm older I can understand why it was down in that area, there are some good water sources and just on the other side of the wood there are allotment gardens full of food. I have found a number of other people who have heard strange howls and growls in this area, I once found a bare footprint in January in the frost that was really large.

The Ivy Den Creature, It had Red Eyes. 1980's - Witness Report: Dave: *"I would like to report something that happened many years ago when I was much younger when I was about 9 or10 years old. We used to play in the old Hackenthorpe woods and we would make dens and swings and stuff out there and just play all day long. One day in the holidays we were in what we called the "ivy den" at Hackenthorpe in Sheffield. I was sitting on a tree higher up than the swing over a stream, I was just sitting there watching everybody when suddenly my friends and my brother got up and ran across the stream and up the bank then off as fast as they could go without saying a word to me.*

I'm just sat hanging on the branch not knowing why they ran and whether I should just sit here and wait? When I looked down the stream to see what could have spooked them or a reason for why they ran, I saw a 6-7 ft dark figure with the brightest red eyes and it was running up the side of the stream about 20 feet away coming in my direction fast. Then this "thing" jumped across the stream with ease (which was too wide for anything normal to jump) and it was heading straight towards me. I dropped off the swing as fast as I could and legged it, running hard. Then I fell trying to get up the banking and as I turned to see where "It" was and it just stood at the other side of the stream staring straight at me. I set off shouting "HELP!"

When my friend heard me yelling thankfully he came back in there and got me and helped me to get out, not my Brother though he was off home without me. During the 1-2 minutes this was happening "It" never made a sound, no thumping of running feet or no sound of a thud or thump when it jumped and landed, this was my second sighting of this "thing" and I can't talk about that second encounter yet and I have also seen a dark figure quite a few times since at work and while out driving, "It" was up the side bank to the side of my car using the bush and shrubs to hide in".

A very short walk away from both of the accounts in the area there is another report that you may find of interest?

Eyes in the Wood, 2014 - This account came into to me by a member of the paranormal community. Witness Report. A.N: *"This is the area I had my sighting, it was a night time sighting and we had just finished a paranormal investigation at this location. We were all walking back to the cars which were about 20 minutes* walk away from where we currently were. We all saw a glowing pair of eyes looking at us from the trees. They were staring at us and it was easy to see they were not a bird's eyes, nor a fox as the eyeshine was too tall to be an animal.

The whole incident really creeped us out at the time. I have since been back to this place and can confirm from a daylight visit where "It" was stood, there is a huge gap between the tree line and the ground and the tree closest to where the eyes would have been has no low branches or anything that a bird could've sat on. The path we used is on a disused railway track that is left to nature and all overgrown there is also a flowing river, and there area has a disused mine (it was this mine we were planning on investigating) I will be going back to document this area and do a follow up investigation."

Children Report A Tree Shaking Creature Doncaster - Witness Report. Neil: "It was near Doncaster that my experience happened on a normal day. There were a few of us children playing out that day and like most of us back then Neil was out with his mates in the woods close to where he lived. The kids he was out with noticed a strange "creature" that at that point had not noticed them. It was shaking a small sapling back and forth. Being kids and not being scared by it, they watched it in curiosity as children do for some time.

They were all laying down in the long grass and as they watched this "creature" continued shaking the tree - it must have sensed them watching because at that point "It"turned around, staring in their direction and realizing "It" was being watched "It" then just wandered off into the woods. It didn't run or seem scared or angry *in any way. It just slowly walked back into the treeline and we just forgot about it and carried on playing. Now I'm an adult, I have no explanation of what happened that day or what this "thing" was to be honest."*

It would seem to me that this area of Yorkshire is a hot spot of sighting reports, the children watching the tree shaking creature could have crossed a few fields and woods and ran into this report of a Green Man face reported by two other children who had also skipped school.

The Green Man Face In The Grass. Bawtry, Summer 1972 - Witness Report. Jo: *"This is what happened to me one summer's afternoon when I was playing out as a child in Bawtry Doncaster, I saw something so strange that the experience remains with me to this day. The face in the foliage that I (and a school friend) saw happened around the time I was 15 in I would say approximately 1972. My Friend and I were playing truant from school, and we knew we wouldn't be caught if we went to a certain area not really ideal but it was out of the way and no adults would see us, we were there messing about in an old abandoned sewage works, known locally as "dead-dogs island" we noticed a face watching us from within the brambles, "he/she" was lying flat on their belly, keeping hidden well in the bushes and grass so I couldn't see a body and I have no idea of the size or height but what we could see was the face, whatever this "thing" was it was hairy and looked like the Green Man pictures and artworks that you see in the UK.*

It seemed to me at the time it was as if he had foliage on his face or was using foliage and greenery to mask his face and hide in plain sight, his skin was dark. He had small dark eyes and he was just looking at us observing what we were doing. My friend was really scared and frightened but I was more interested, it looked like the foliage was being used to disguise his face somehow or it was a mask made from the grass and leaves? He didn't try to move or approach us and we ran off and he didn't try to follow us either he just stayed in position as far as I know he just stayed in the brambles. I can still remember the incident as clear as day. I wasn't scared and I really wanted to know more but my friend running left me there alone with "him" so I quickly followed her out of there.

In the same area within a year of my first encounter myself and my Brother were walking home and we realised we were being followed by something we couldn't see in the trees and bushes off to the left of us. It was a dark night and we caught a glimpse of something that had orangish eyes and whatever this thing was it growled at us from the bushes in almost the same area".

The Green Man

The Milton Campsie "Poacher" 2016 - Witness Report. J. H:
"*Deborah after seeing your work at BBR and the research you have done on the "British Bigfoot" and the Woodwose and the fact that you are based in the UK, I feel comfortable sharing my experience with you, I have not shared it online before as to be honest I didn't have a clue where to report this to. This all happened one day, it was the beginning of August of last year and I was out walking with my son in the small woodland close to my house. I stay in a small village called Milton of Campsie, and we were out that day well off the beaten track, it's a pretty old set of woods with 200-300 + year old trees.*

Nothing out of the ordinary happened at first but we were quite a ways in there when about 15 -20 yards in front of us what I thought was a Poacher in a Ghillie suit, this "Poacher" stood up and started to make his way at a good pace away from us moving swiftly, "he" was moving quickly and not looking back in our direction, given at the time of day I was sure this was a poacher. I wanted to confront him as I was angry at the fact that someone would be firing a gun or a bow so close to where people walk with their families and dogs etc.

I decided to give him a piece of my mind so I set off after him, as I got closer he rounded the back of an old Oak Tree and was gone, completely vanished. I couldn't see him anywhere, at this point given I was still thinking it was a poacher I shouted out loud, and believe me I ranted loud enough so that if he had gone to ground he would still hear me as I was pretty angry by this point.

But I heard a strange rumbling sound at the time which sounded kinda like a big tree was ready to come down and it was coming from the Oak Tree the "poacher" had gone behind. But I played it down to nothing given the fact I often hear weird stuff all the time in the woods that I can't explain so I brushed it off until I got home.

I never did find "him" and it wasn't until later that day I was telling my father about what had happened earlier and he mentioned so matter of factly that I'd most likely seen the "Greenman" now this is the first time I've ever heard this name in connection with the forests, but everyone I talk to now is so matter of fact about it, as if it isn't so strange at all. So needless to say I spend every spare minute I can in the woods now, not to prove anything to anyone more to see what I can find for myself."

Ghillie Suit

Two Boys See A Huge Hairy Muscled Creature In Tarleton Lancs
1996 - Witness Report. Mark Farnell: I was contacted in 2016 by a gentleman who wished to report his account of something that happened to him and his friend when they were young boys living in the Tarleton Area of Lancashire. As most of us did back then, a day in the local woods would bring us a lot of joy and excitement, on this occasion they got a little more excitement than they initially planned. Whilst playing amongst the trees they noticed a strange "*hunched hairy creature*" watching them.

"Back in July of 1996, when I was 13 years of age, my friend and I witnessed something in the local woods that lie close to the small village I lived in that to this very day I can not explain. I have tried to work out what I saw and like many people in the UK who have seen a similar thing I can only describe it as an "Ape like human looking creature covered in hair".

We were only young kids back then and just messing about and entertaining ourselves as kids do, we would go down there often and that day was no different at first. If only we had known that day was going to be very strange and decades later the day would be imprinted on my mind. We had just completed building an assault course through the woods off track with rope swings etc. We gave it a try out from start to finish and we were running the course and making a racket but we both noticed something vague and hard to describe that came walking through the brush ahead of us, not more than 15 feet away. We didn't Know what "it" was and we had never seen anything like it before.

We watched as "it" came walking into a clearing. This "thing" was broad but it wasn't much taller than us at the time, perhaps only

5/5 ft but its body was huge, "It" was hairy and thick with muscle. I remember "It" having a humped back almost, it was sort of stooped somehow, it was walking with purpose and then "It" just stopped?

At the time my friend and I looked at each other knowing what we were seeing was wordless. Even now I'm struggling to describe what "It" looked like and what it felt like to me standing there looking at "It" and wondering what "It" was going to do next. We started to back off until we felt like it was "OK" to pick up the pace. As we looked back we noticed it was trying to focus on us through the trees, keeping a watch on us and where we were heading? And at that moment "It" let out a blood curdling grunt/scream. It was a terrifying noise. Up until that point I kept telling myself it was just an adult or some strange looking person, but that scream changed that. Knowing it wasn't a person we ran away even quicker than ever. Through fear I have never been back to the local woods. It all happened in Tarleton Village, Lancashire UK.

The "creature" had long dark grey and light brown matted hair. "It" was hairy and thick with muscle. And I will never forget that day."

Mark has become a close friend over the years, as with many of the people I meet when you recognise the same questions being asked by you both, the same confusion being felt and the constant *"why did I have to see it"* it's like finding a long lost twin and the relief is enormous. Mark has gone on to help other witnesses to creatures we can't name and paranormal events and is in the process of completing his first Documentary on the subject. He is also the artist behind many of the images I use in my blogs and books.

Mark did return to the area years later to revisit as many of us do, but like me he isn't too keen on repeating the visit. I lived in quite an urban area and had a lot of streets to hide behind, sadly Tarleton is an area that is heavily farmed for food and cattle, with a small village surrounded by wooded pockets, streams and fields, it would of been much harder for Mark growing up around there than it was for the "inner city" witnesses.

Not too far away from Mark's sighting and within an easy jog is another account of a strange creature by the roadside.

Hunched Figure by the Road Side, 1993 - One of the sources of witness accounts are the hundreds of researchers we have all across the UK, looking for accounts online in forums and groups or checking Youtube for any video that may mention a creature or a strange experience, some of the researchers also ask people on the woodland meets for information or leads to track down and this account came in when one of the researchers was explaining what we do here in the research team and how easy it was to join in and meet the witnesses and other people with a similar interest.

"I was talking to one of my neighbours about my hobby and what I do for the team and about the accounts we receive from everywhere. I had just told him about some accounts in the area and he remembered something that had happened to him when he was much younger and was visiting relatives in the Manchester area. The couple he stayed with had travelled to Blackpool to show

him the sights and it was on the return journey that this incident happened.

He stated "I get a little confused as it was so long ago now and I'd forgotten all about it until you said about the road crossing creature. I do know it was winter time and we were driving on a part of the dual carriageway between Manchester and Blackpool. It was dark, of course but the road was well lit.

We had been around Blackpool and looked at the lights and as we were driving back home I noticed something out of the corner of my eye. I looked to the side of the road and saw a Figure standing there out of place, "It" was all black 6 to 7 feet tall, bigger than a man and "It" was kind of hunched over. "It" was pretty big and bulky but we couldn't make out too many details,"It" was just standing at the side of the road looking like "It" was thinking about crossing. It didn't move as we passed "it" as we looked back it had gone? And we couldn't see where it would have gone too"?

The Cleadon Geet, NE 2002/3 - *"I am not sure of the exact year this happened but I am 33 now, and what happened took place when I was age 16. I'm from Whitburn and had been to see my girlfriend who lived in East Boldon, it is a bit of a walk so I usually caught the bus home. The last bus was around 11pm, and I often used to miss it. Then I'd have to walk home, which took around an hour, so I set off in hopes of catching it.*

I always followed a well used route along Cleadon Lane, a dark country road heading into Whitburn that was a bit overgrown and you couldn't see clearly at night on either side of you. On one occasion there was a clear sky and the moonlight was shining, not a full moon, but enough so that it wasn't pitch black and I could see up ahead as I was walking along heading to the bus stop. About 100 metres up from the Charlie Hurley Centre, next to the sign for Whitburn, I was caught short and needed to use the bushes as a bathroom, I stopped to pee and moved over towards the bushes, so I wasn't visible to anyone coming along the road or out of the woods.

To my complete shock as I'm answering a call of nature the bushes open up in front of me, they just parted and this massive, skinny, hairy "thing" came lunging out at me. I jumped back, and remembered screaming in shock because it was so tall and hairy. I can only describe it as looking like Chewbacca from Star Wars but thinner. It scared me witless, I turned and ran quicker than I'd ever ran before, and I could hear its thuds behind me for maybe 10 metres. It clearly did not want me there, I didn't stop to look back and my feet didn't touch the deck. I was running for my life I thought, I can honestly say I would have beaten Linford Christie at that moment in time. I never stopped until I got home, which was next to the Army camp. I did tell people, over and over, I never shut up for weeks about it to my friends, half who believed me (because I wasn't a story-teller, like some) and half who laughed and didn't believe me!

I returned on my bike the next day and tried to piece together what had happened. and I noticed that the bushes went down into a ditch, and I worked out from the size of the ditch, that the thing must have been up to 7ft tall.

As the years have passed some people still bring my experience up and chuckle about it, but when I saw your article, I ripped it out and showed a lot of them. They couldn't believe it. What they no doubt struggled with was the fact that the more people who claimed to have seen the creature, the less likely it was that the beast was imaginary, as opposed to very real".

But a growing number of people have claimed to see the Geet, and no matter how bizarre or unbelievable it might seem we are forced to take seriously what they say.

Another report from a short walk away on exactly the same road another visitor to the area is also referring to his sighting of this creature they call the "Geet."

The Cleadon Wildman 6/10/03 - *"I was in Cleadon in the North East when I encountered what seemed to be a large bipedal creature. I was visiting a friend who lives in the area, when I decided to walk to the local store to purchase some wine to supplement the meal she was about to cook for us.*

The night was dark so it is hard to tell exactly the description of this "creature" however "It" appeared to have a thick fur coat. I estimate that I was around 50 yards from the "creature" as "It" walked along the edge of a tree line, before "It" was startled and ran back into the trees.

I only came to be walking in the area as a shortcut between a colleagues house and the local store. I have been on various websites looking for other sightings in this area but have so far been fruitless in my search for a similar encounter. It was solidly built, with what looked like a thick fur coat on.

The encounter was very brief so unfortunately there is not much else to report, although there was another person in the vicinity at the time. I believe they were taking their dog for a walk (which is possibly what startled the creature) although by the time I had walked around the waterlogged area between myself and the person, they had gone along the same route as the creature I saw".

Strange Experiences At Home, Growls And Howls In The Night - Witness Report. Liam: *"I contacted you as I have been experiencing some strange howls and noises close to home and I wondered if any of your readers had experienced anything of a similar nature. I'd say the first time I had ever noticed anything I would have been about 10-11 yrs old, it was just after I'd gone to bed in the summer and there were dogs barking everywhere along the streets and I was at my window listening to all the noise and commotion, after around half an hour of it starting all the barking stopped suddenly and I could hear a faint howl that sounded as if it was kind of distorted. Not a howl you would expect to hear like foxes or dogs, this howl was really strange.*

So I went and got my Mum so she too could listen to it and tell me what it was. She stood at the window with me smirking at first as if she was just going along with it to humour me as I was young, but then she heard it herself and her face immediately dropped and she quickly said "Oh it's nothing" I almost believed her but as soon as she said it she went all the way around the house checking that the doors were locked and closing all of the curtains. This might have been at around 9 pm because I remember it being around summer time and it was still pretty light outside.

The second time was quite a long while after as I'm 21 now and I started to notice things again late last year (2017) around September time. It had started with minor things such as what I can only describe as hearing what sounded like a dustbin being dragged down the street at a ridiculous speed, then later in the night there were obvious sounds of things being thrown and hitting the wire fence on the field across the road from my house. I could hear the horses in the field sounding like they were petrified and stampeding around.

There were two nights where there was some really long drawn out groaning sounds that would get closer to the house and then fade away, and this would repeat and then get closer again, both times they'd persist for around for about an hour, maybe slightly longer but during that time every animal including the usually very loud dogs in the street were completely silent? When the noise stopped it seemed like every animal was in panic mode, or shaken up somehow?

One thing I will mention but I'm not entirely sure if it has a reasonable explanation or not is a night in August last year, I could hear a toddler murmuring outside on the street as if it were upset and I shrugged it off because the folk across the road often have their grand kids round and they are usually playing in the garden at daft times till late. After I had tried to ignore it for probably 10 minutes it went from murmuring to absolutely stomach churning screaming, It didn't sound like kids playing at this point so I jumped out of bed and got dressed, I grabbed the bar we use to open and close the loft hatch without even realising and I ran outside thinking some child was being hurt or abducted? The moment that I got outside it stopped, everything was deadly silent, no-one was around, and that's when it hit me about hearing from people with Dogman and Bigfoot encounters, where the creature may imitate sounds of children in distress or shout your name to lure people outside?

But at that point I put that out of my mind and I tried to rationalise the experience and I ran up and down at least five different streets looking for whatever made the noise and I saw nobody, and I didn't see anyone who had come outside because they heard the racket too? There wasn't even a house with its lights on with people looking out of the windows or twitching the curtains, it was deadly silent. The next day I asked my parents about what had happened in the night and they didn't even know I'd gone out of the house, let alone heard a kid screaming. Which I thought was strange because I literally burst out of my room and sprinted down the stairs not caring about making noise or waking anyone up. I have a recording of the "groaning" type noise. I would be interested in knowing what people think it was because I have no idea at all?

I live in an area where there is plenty of wooded places etc and we have a lot of water sources around here and plenty of dykes and brooks deep enough for probably something the size of a horse to move along in undetected by most people. Also, the area near my house where the noises seem to have been emanating from has now been designated a nature reserve and they've gone to quite an effort to keep people out. I will make sure to wander around the area and see if I can make out any signs or just to see if I see anything unusual."

Another account that reports strange noise of children crying is the Weeping Figure of Evesham featured in this book, but I would like to add an account of howling that is hard to explain away, there are not many creatures that howl or whoop here in the UK.

The Tilmanstone Strange Whoops, Sept 2015 - *"I wrote to you as I have heard something really weird while I was working, I'm a carpet fitter so I travel from house to house fitting carpets or giving quotations. I had a job out in the way out in the sticks as we call it. I was unloading some underlay from my van I heard about four really loud unusual vocalizations? Now the best way I can describe these sounds were like a "Whooing" noise four single howl's emitted one at a time, not a noise I would usually hear on a normal day at work and for all we were out in the country it wasn't anything I could think of, these"Whoo's" really stood out they sounded like the sort of "whoo" you would hear in a Jungle.*

They did however sound like the noise a primate would make somewhere far away and tropical. Yet the nearest zoo is 25 miles away. I wouldn't think sound would travel that far but I might be wrong? I've never heard these noises before and it was enough for me to stop in my tracks and really listen to what direction it was coming from. I was in the Tilmanstone area of Kent which is an old mining village near the Dover Sandwhich area.

I listened really hard to clue into how far away this sound was and I did it for a while, they sounded close but not close at the same time, I couldn't not pin point a direction and I knew it wasn't a fox or anything like that. To be honest as I was in work mode frame of mind and thinking about the job ahead I think that's why it stood out so much as I could tell it was nothing I had heard before, If I had to state what kind of noise I would have to say it was definitely like a primate type of whoop, it sounded like a very haunting sound it sort of hung in the air after it finished. It wouldn't have sounded out of place in a jungle type environment but in the middle of Kent it did which makes it very hard one to explain".

The Tiny Weeping Figure, A Crying Creature. Evesham, 1980's-Witness Report. T Roberts: "*I contacted you as I would like to tell you about my experience that happened around the age of 14/15 years. I am not too sure as it was an experience that I've tried to put it out of my mind, but failed miserably too forget. Making me seek information over 20 years later and find myself now writing this story for you. Late one night I was walking the usual route. I would walk on my way home something I had done hundreds of times before. it was around 10/11pm, as a youngster I was allowed out later than the majority of my friends due to the lack of good parenting at home. On this route I had to pass a small area of disused and very overgrown land, thick of brambles, trees, bushes and overgrown grass etc. The area is just off the River Avon and the walk always gave me the creeps at this time of night, seeing as the "spooky" area was on the right hand side of the road it always made me veer off over to the left side as I felt a little safer there. I made my way to the opposite footpath and out of the corner of my eye I could see a largish "bulk" directly beneath the lamp post, that made me look harder as this type of thing was never usually there.*

To my astonishment and disbelief I saw what seemed to be an animal of some sort as this "thing" had rugged hair everywhere and I could see its body kind of raising up and down to the motion of "some one/thing" breathing. What seemed really odd was the fact this creature appeared to be standing on its hind legs, and was standing about little over one metre high (not large at all for a "yeti/bigfoot" or any animal really) and "it" was standing with its back towards me, but I still just couldn't figure out how this animal was stood upright so easily, at which point and I have no idea why I started to quietly approach the figure thinking that my eyes really must be deceiving me and kind of hoping it to be just some old shaggy rug that somebody had left out and wanting to de-bunk any silly ideas I was getting in my head I kept moving forward. Originally I must have been around 30 metres away when I first saw the "thing" I had advanced towards the creature questioning my eyes the whole way, with my heart beating faster and faster the closer I became, my mind racing faster and faster releasing this was no dog, no rug, and certainly couldn't possibly be a small child in some kind of halloween costume. Whatever "It" was "It" was definitely an alive animal that stood easily on its hind legs.

The closer I got I started to hear its breathing and a kind of snuffling that was recognisable, at this point I had left as little as 4-5 metres between myself and "It." As my mind raced, all I could see and hear was as clear as day (being directly beneath a lit lamp post) but I was still finding it difficult for my mind to take all this in as right before me was this strange creature and what seemed even more crazy was the fact that it actually appeared to be crying/sulking exactly like you might expect a small child to do. I could see (as I was close enough) that it actually had its right arm upwards with its forearm against its forehead with its body tipped forward towards the lampost using it to lean against or even hide its head/face into the exact same way small children do, its body *juddered up and down quickly with every snorting/snuffling sound it was creating, again the same way a child might do. My mind was astounded, almost in shock as I stood there for what seemed like an eternity, but was probably just a matter of seconds. As my brain started to catch up with itself I started to imagine what its face might look like, and what its reaction might be if "It" were to catch me standing so close.*

At this point complete fear had started to take over my mind and body, as all I could picture in my mind was that it would have teeth, as large and pointy as a dogs teeth and that it probably wouldn't take too kindly to me having accidently sneaked up upon "It. I could imagine "It" turning to face me, getting angry and most likely attacking me. (Of course my mind had begun to run away with itself beyond any control). I haven't actually seen its face or teeth, but I really did not like being that close just in case. To which my feet started backing off without me even releasing I was moving, I went extremely quietly and extremely slowly not daring to make any sound, not even a breath, although I swear it could have heard my heart thumping away so hard in my chest that I could feel it almost make my head pulsate with every beat.

Fearing it would turn around with every backwards step I took, placing my feet with very direct careful placements, trying not to accidently scuff my feet. I dared not take my wide open eyes off "It" not even for a second until I met with my original path home, at which point I slowly disappeared around the corner out of its direct view. Still not daring to make any noise possible and quite literally sneaking the rest of the way, I carefully began my short walk home continually looking over my shoulder making sure I had not been seen and was not being followed. Even when I got home I carefully shut the front door still not wanting to make any noise, still stricken with fear, but at last I could take a long deep breath of relief, finally being able to breathe properly since the first sign of panic had kicked in. Also in relief of the creature having not seen or heard me.

I'm a rather rational person, who would never usually believe in any silly stories or so I thought. I'm much more scientific minded even to this day, but I cannot deny what my eyes and other senses had seen, heard and felt that night. Whatever "It" was this "creature" had longish brown fur which I remember moved in the occasional gentle gust of wind, I remember seeing the outline of "Its" body, "It's" legs, and curiously "It's" arm positions. My mind still even too this day still finds it hard to believe that whatever this thing was, "It" had expressed signs of human emotion...it actually was crying/sulking! Its whole body language told me that even the noises that it had created were child like only this was definitely no child and to my knowledge no monkey. "It's" shape and stature was completely different. It seemed to closely resemble a small child but much bulkier.

In a way at times I wish I hadn't seen it, as I don't want anybody to ever think I may create fairy tale-like stories, as I despise anybody that would ever make up any story like this. I'd chosen to keep my story to myself, telling only the one or two very close friends that I know would know me enough not to have ever created any fictional stories of any sort. Don't get me wrong, I've seen my fair share of strange goings on, but all could be explained away rationally, or to have been created by some natural or manmade means possibly.

But not this, I know all I had seen that night was no trickery of any sort and that I would never be able to prove my story, at least not until some kind of evidence is found. I await that day with the knowledge that I know "something" IS out there. whether it be "Alien" "Bigfoot" or whether it be some kind of other "creature" that has been able to hide from man for many years now. But the fact remains. I KNOW IT IS OUT THERE SOMEWHERE and to this day and in the future, I will never forget what I had experienced that night in question".

Less than 4 mile away from this encounter with the strange weeping "creature" we have a gentleman who tells of an experience whilst out with a metal detector in the fields and woods one night. And another couple who see small figures in the road way.

"Little Thick Bodied Hairy Men that Moved Really Fast Across the Road." - Witness Report. P/JN: *"I have a story for you that was told to me by a fellow I met who goes out metal detecting at night, so he can move around without being seen because he hasn't got permission from the landowner. He was out late on night metal detecting on Bredon Hill in Worcestershire with his mate. He was walking along in the dark, swinging his detector, one ear in the headphones listening for "hits"and one ear to the night. His mate was detecting alongside him just a little further down the field, when they got to the end of the field that then turned into woods he stopped, but his mate carried on and went further into the woods. He thought this was strange and wondered what he was doing?*

He could hear his footsteps in the wood and called out, "Any good in there?" or something like that. There was no answer. A bit puzzled, he turned to make his way back up the field where they had started from, when he caught sight of his mate's cigarette end glowing and bobbing around further up the field. This is when he realised that whatever or whoever it was that had been walking alongside him and then carried on into the woods was not his mate".

Slitting Mill Three Hairy Things 1975-98 - Witness Report. Barry & Elaine: Mentioned in a Staffordshire blog is this very strange story of little creatures from 1975 The tale begins with an introduction to a young couple called Barry and Elaine who are coming home from a Christmas party in the early hours of the morning with their two children tucked up warm asleep in the back seat and they are driving towards their home in Slitting Mill. The car they were driving in stalled and Barry, who back then was in his twenties got out of the car to go and check the engine over, he messed around with a few spark plugs and eventually fixed it luckily without too much trouble and while he was returning to his wife in the car she saw 'something' that the then young couple later described as 'trolls'.

According to Barry, "*Elaine let out a loud scream, terrified by the sight of a small figure that ran across the road in front of them at a high rate of speed. She explains: "I just about saw it at the last second, and then another one followed it, and then a third one. The best way I can describe them to you is like a hairy troll or something like that. Little thick bodied hairy men that moved really fast across the road. We had some moonlight that night so it was easy to see them and they were like little men, but with hunchbacks and big hooked crooked noses and not a stitch of cloth on them at all. Nothing covered the bodies, just hair and it was all over them.*

I would say they were all four-feet-tallish, and when the third one crossed by us, you could see them at the edge of the trees – wary, or something, as if not wanting to enter the woods for some reason?

Things then became very confusing, Barry says: "We both know from memory that they came forwards, towards us, taking small steps very slowly to us, and I've thought since that day that they were interested in us or wanted to know who we were. They came very slowly, and it felt a bit like we were being hunted, or stalked, to me. Elaine was hysterical; and with the kids with us, I wasn't far-off either. Did we see a little wildman"?

I am not entirely sure what the couple saw that day and the whole account would be lost in time if not for some further unusual incidents that happened.

Slitting Mill is very close to Cannock Chase, an area with around 28 sighting reports. From Werewolves to Pigman the Chase is an area of very strange energy.

In 1995 a very quick sighting was made of a huge hair covered creature by a witness named Jackie Houghton. Jackie explained she saw *"a huge and lumbering hair-covered creature"* in the early hours of the morning near the small, picturesque village of Slittingmill Staffordshire, which is interestingly in the heart of the Chase. Cannock Chase is a hotbed of paranormal events and creature encounters from headless horsemen to the British

Bigfoot and many a Werewolf too. And then a further event was added as little as three short years later.

In 1998, the following account surfaced from another witness online who shared their encounter on the Chase: *"It was a star filled night and easy to see by, it was clear but still dark and we were all in the car driving home, we were just happily chatting and joking with each other when suddenly we all fell dead serious, without saying anything the mood changed really quickly. There were a couple of people sitting in the back and they all sat forward and we all pointed to the same shape at the same time.*

It was a tall man-like figure and "he" was sort of crouching forward in a strange position. As we passed "him" in the car "It" turned and looked straight at us. In my own words I would describe "It" as around six feet eight inches tall with legs thicker than two of mine, "It" was very strong looking and had a darkish, blacky [sic]-brown coat. I just could not explain "It" to you clearly at all and I still get goosebumps thinking about it."

As we know Staffordshire itself is home to many strange creature reports, we only have to look at Cannock Chase and the surrounding areas to see that something is being seen and reported on a regular basis. Although I feel Cannock is researched out, hundreds of cryptozoologists and paranormal groups abound at the Castle Ring, I do think the areas just a little way out, the smaller woods where there are also many accounts of creatures and beasts galore, are more than likely place to be looking for signs, many of the accounts mention road crossing creatures or creatures alongside the car, so if your bored this weekend and in the area maybe a drive will relieve the boredom, and get the blood pumping if your in the right place at the right time.

A Strange Creature On The Golf Course Salford, 2016 - Witness Report. J. Lewis: *"I came across your blog while I was looking for the Finding Bigfoot Website or somewhere I could report this experience too, and when I saw your site and the witness statements I thought you would want to hear about the strange "Beast" my husband saw last month on the Golf course.*

He was golfing at the Ellesmere golf course in Worsley. While doing the round he was on the side of the course where the trees separate the course from the East Lancashire road. While he and his friend were playing they noticed something walking along the edge of the treeline. They thought for a moment it was another golfer but after about ten minutes or so they became aware that this "thing" was walking with them, copying their pace and steps and they got the impression that it was stalking them?

They looked closer and saw that whatever "It" was the "thing" they were looking at was very tall, around about 7ft. It was hairy all over the body and the "thing" was human shaped. They also said "It" had a "barrelled chest and was very large with an odd shaped head" "It looked like a human but wider and with hair covering it all over" "The way "It" leaned forward the men felt that "It" was either very old or in some sort of pain or had an affliction of some kind. As they looked at "It" they heard It" making a muttering sound like something chattering, like the sounds an ape would make.

My husband stepped forward towards the "creature" and "It" took a step back away from him. When "It" did this the muttering stopped and "It" went quiet. My husband's friend walked towards "It" and "It" started to sway from side to side, and they got the impression "It" was getting agitated as they got closer and closer. "It" clapped "It's" hands very loudly and started making grunting sounds. My husband noticed "It's" hands were very big, almost too big for its arms, he described the arms and hands almost like "bedpans" in comparison to our hand size. He said "It" then started moving its hands, a little like sign language, gesturing. Then suddenly they heard a loud wailing coming from another part of the trees and at that moment the creature turned and ran away, again making this odd grunting sound.

I don't expect you to believe this story but I swear it is true. My husband didn't want to report it but I heard that Finding Bigfoot came to England and spoke to you. So I thought they may want to come here to see the spot where it happened. But I found this blog and all the similar sightings so thought I would contact you instead. Maybe you can shed some light on what he saw?

My husband and his friends are very down to earth rational men, but John was as white as a sheet when he came home, he has played golf round these parts for years and years, so to see this was just shocking for him, he was so shaken up I thought at first he had come across some trouble or mither (annoyance or repeated interruption) from someone down on the course, when he explained what had happened I believed everything he said, I had to make him a sweet drink of tea to calm him down."

Thank you John and Jade Lewis for this account.

This sighting is of great interest to me, as the encounter I had as a child was less than 3 miles as the crow flies from my experience at Buile Hill, I know this as I ran the entire way home that day. Salford is not the sort of town for myths and fables, legends and tales, it's a hard working class town, where you get your head down, do your bit, be nice to your neighbours, in the way of most small British towns. What people fail to realise as you reach the outskirts of the built up area, there are miles and miles of fields and golf courses, Clifton Country Park and Drinkwater lead up to the pennines, and the forest of Bowland. There are a number of creature and ape man accounts running North to South skirting the Manchester area.

The Haslingden Hairy man, Peeping Around The Door - Witness. U. N: *"This incident took place in Haslingden, Lancashire, though the witness was only 17 at the time she still remembers it like yesterday. When she describes the creature as standing in the kitchen/dining area doorway, and nearly as tall as the door frame, we are naturally assuming that she was saying the creature stood in a back door that led outside into the back garden. "This is a thing I don't tell people it's something I keep to myself. I may sound mad but when I was about 17 I lived in Haslingden in Lancashire.*

My Mum and Dad were out and I was on the phone which was usual when my parents went out, back then it was the old rotary phone and you felt like you needed "written permission" back then to run up the bill (I think most people in my generation would remember doing this too). I was sitting on the phone cabinet and idly looking around the room chatting away when I looked towards the kitchen/dining room and there was a person looking at me through the door. "He" (it felt like a he?) looked like Chewbacca I suppose. His head reached only an inch or two from the top of the door frame and he'd sort of poked his head and upper body round the doorway like he was checking who was on the phone. I didn't feel threatened (except of course 'it wasn't supposed to be there!).

Honestly it seems more like he was curious to see who it was he could hear. We looked at each other for about five seconds. It's a bloody long time. I don't remember anything unusual about his eyes, they were not glowing or red or anything like that. He was a sort of mousy blonde haired. Then either he left or I freaked out and looked away. My friend on the phone was panicking because I'd gone silent mid-sentence. I was too scared to tell her what I'd seen but I made her stay on the phone till my parents came home. Dad went into the kitchen when he got in but there was nothing there.

I didn't tell any of my family and never saw him again. I've no idea what any of this is. How would something that big get into my house? Maybe this didn't help you at all. By the way it was about 7.45pm (Top of the Pops was on!) and it was sometime in October. I hadn't been drinking or had any experience at all with drugs. Anyway, hope this helps in some way."

There is also a strange account that was reported very close to this encounter in 2016 in the Helmshore area.

Helmshore Heavy Walker, Homeless Man Disturbed In The Night, Autumn 2016 - There comes a time for all of us, when life seems to fight you and your luck turns bad, and it can even sometimes make you homeless and this account comes from a witness called Alan and at the time of his experience he had nowhere to stay, with his two Dogs and a tent he made a home here for the time being in the hope of finding work and setting down some roots.

He had set up his tent and camp as best he could and had settled in, and for a few nights everything was fine, he was just off the river, and he didn't see anybody and figured he would be ok here until the weather turned really bad. It wasn't such a bad place to be after all, until that all changed.

Although he never saw what bothered him night after night, and what made him feel watched day after day, what made the knocks on trees and snapped branches and launched them in to his camp area, he was never brave enough to go and look, for as he described it, *"it seemed to be walking in such a way as to make me aware it was there, loud thumping feet in the leaves*, rustling that was louder than any small animal could make, things moved when I was away from the camp and it was clear *"something"* had been through his things, nothing was missing and a few times I could feel eyes on me as he zipped up for the night, but around 1am something wood come to camp approaching from the south east, whatever was moving around was walking noises like it was on two feet not walking or scurrying like an animal would, and although described with the similar bulkiness of a Cow, this thing was much heavier and sounded much larger but never came within eyesight.

Whatever it was stayed within the trees. His two Dogs never made a sound when "It" was around and as they were Staffordshire Bull Terriers they were more than capable of seeing to themselves, but they didn't want to leave the tent until Alan did each morning. After too many nights like this over about a month or so, he used the excuse of Winter to head off into Rossendale and looked for shelter there.

When he was interviewed by a family member of mine one sunday morning Alan came looking for me but sadly I couldn't travel to see him so my Father went instead and took the account for me. My father who was no fool said Alan came across as honest and puzzled and a little scared by the experience, he had not heard of the "British bigfoot or any Cryptid until he was able to look online and search for similar encounters. Alan said *"he was ex army and not easily spooked but that he just had something happen that he could not explain. "If I thought it was a person I would have just* moved them on, but what I heard was no person. His closing reply was "there is something huge moving around in the trees up there, I'm just glad I didn't see it."

Thetford Walking Figure In The Dark And Something Crossing The Lane, June 2017 - Witness Report: "*I live quite close to Thetford Forest and have over the years had a couple of strange experiences whilst out in the Forest itself and I wanted to share them with you. The first thing that happened to me happened when I stayed outdoors overnight by the river Little Ouse. We had cayaked upstream from Santon Downham until we reached the weir and river gauging station. We drifted back downstream a little to a suitable location to pull the canoe out of the water and with suitable trees strong enough to set up our hammocks for the night. We walked until we were far off the beaten track and decided we would set up camp for the night in the spot we found. It was about 02:00 hrs when we settled into our hammocks to get some sleep. All was quiet and then we both heard slow and deliberate movement that approached us, we both asked each other at the same time "Is that you?" and we both answered "No, I thought it was you moving?"*

We remained silent and the sound of footsteps circled us before slowly walking away. Whatever "It" was would pause if we made any kind of noise and then start up again if we were quiet? In the first light we could clearly see the trampled down tall grass and the route "It" took to and around us before returning to continue along the river bank. There is no path along the river where we stayed, only tall grass and very vicious stinging nettles that could sting through your jeans. It was all really strange. Someone had walked up to the camp and walked slowly round the hammocks with enough noise we could hear them and then off again along the river.

As we paddled back in the morning we went over what we had seen and heard to try and work out what or who it could've been. It could have been a person but I find it strange they would be walking along an overgrown river bank in the dead of night with no torch or light to guide them? How did they manage not to trip over, fall in the river or not to react to being stung by the nettles? The only thing we could think of was "It" had to walk upright on two legs, this is based on the sound of footsteps and the tracks in the long grass and nettles, plus I have good night vision and we were very aware of our surroundings. I don't think either of us wanted to say exactly what we thought "It" could have been in case "It" put either of us off bushcrafting in the forest. Neither of us felt scared or unsettled at any time while whatever it was investigated in our camp.

The second account happened on the morning of Sunday 25 June 2017: I got up early and decided to take my dog for a good long walk through the forest. I parked my car down a forest track that has right of way with vehicle access permitted. We set off as normal, birds singing, cool air with the warmth of the sun just detectable on the skin. My dog normally walks about 2-3 meters in front when off the lead. She does seem to think that all creatures in the forest are potential play friends. She is also friendly to other people and dogs, she barks or rather yaps excitedly to engage the other dog to engage in "chase me games" I like to think I know her barks and their meanings quite well by now.

The walk goes well with nothing out of the ordinary. We go by a potential overnight bushcraft location and I see a woven willow or hazel screen has been erected at a spot that overlooks the railway line and Little Ouse river valley. The screen has about 4 rectangular apertures at various heights as if for binoculars to be used through. It is too far off the beaten track and marked trails to be for the average visitor. The grass is not trodden down near it so has not been used too much just yet. We carry on and take a shortcut back to the car.

I put the travel harness on my dog and clip her in. Start the car and slowly head down the track to exit the forest. I have the windows down to enjoy the cool breeze and smile at my dog with her head out of the window. All of a sudden her head appears between the two front seats and she is staring at something ahead. Nothing I say or do will break her stare so I begin to scan the track and verge ahead for a person, a dog or deer. I am aware she has now stood up and is leaning forward as if to get a better look or to be in front. I cannot see anything out of place up the track ahead of us but I do slow down to a crawl just in case something should run out in front. All of a sudden she starts barking at full volume.

This is not her greeting bark, it is so much deeper and powerful. In between each bark she now growls and her top lip is curled back showing her teeth. In the 5 years I have owned her she has never ever displayed this behaviour. I stop the car and try to reassure her that everything is okay. She does all she can to keep looking ahead with snarls, growls and deep powerful barking. I like to think I know my dog well but this did unsettle me a little. I decided to carry on driving in the hope of passing whatever is causing her to be so agitated. By now she is pulling against her harness and I have never ever heard the sounds she is making before, I have also never seen her so agitated and focused on what she has decided is a threat. I keep scanning the track ahead and verges but I see nothing out of the ordinary.

As I'm driving I try to keep an eye on her to try and see her turn and face whatever "It" is when we pass by, but also keep one eye on the track ahead. For a moment I consider turning the car around and leaving the forest via the long way out to avoid whatever is the cause of her agitation. Up ahead coming out of the verge of tall grasses, bracken and nettle is "something" moving from left to right. "It's" movements looked fluid and deliberate. My first thought was "It" is a vehicle of some type? But the idea is quickly dismissed as how would "It" fit through the trees and who would "It" be? Before I could get a better look, "It" had crossed the track and I could no longer see "It".

I did not get a chance to have a good look and see detail because of the distance and speed with which "It" crossed the track. "It" was grey/brown in colour with no sharp/defined outline such as a vehicle. My mind is trying to match the image with what "It" could be. My dog is still growling, snarling and barking. As we passed the spot where "It" crossed I could see a parting of the bracken and grass but not like a deer trail that is clearly defined. My dog is now facing the way the creature has gone, her hackles up, snarling, growling, deep barking and in a wide defensive stance. She then faces out the rear still barking until we get on the main road and head home. I still have no idea what crossed that path and upset the dog so much, but she has never acted this way before.

*I was meant to be spending tonight wild camping in the forest
close to the sighting area but I have decided to give it a miss for
the time being. I am tempted to return to the area tomorrow and
have a good exploration, maybe take some photos or video for
reference so I can track any changes? I will bring my dog (on the
lead) with me for two reasons, firstly for company and secondly to
see if she reacts and gives me a warning to remove myself and her
from the area.*

Thetford Forest as we know is a hotbed of creatures, baboons,
bear men and other strange upright figures that roam the woods
of trees of the Forest.

I was contacted by a gentleman who said something happened to
him when he was much younger that up until now he had no
explanation for, a hairy gorilla like creature in an English garden is
not something this gentleman thought other people would have
seen too, I advised him there are many witnesses and I would
happily share his account in the hopes somebody in the area saw
something similar back then, before this event or after. Or anyone
in the UK who has seen a similar type creature. This is the
Gentleman's account in his own words:

A Young Boy Sees A Peeping Gorilla And Screams In The Night.
Springwell NE - Witness Report. J. M: *"Deborah, do you have any
accounts in the Springwell Area in the North East of England? The
reason I ask is when I was younger around 12 or 13 I would sleep
over at my grandparents a lot during the weekends and school
holidays and one night when I was staying over and I saw what
looked like a gorilla's head peeking out from behind a tree in the
garden and looking through the trees outside my window, I think it*

was watching me in bed and I remember being so scared I hid under the covers for the rest of the night worried this "gorilla" would climb in the window and get me.

If I had to describe it I would say, "The face kind of just looked like a gorilla, with not much hair on the face, this "thing" had a short stubby nose, with massive eyes that looked black but it was dark so I'm not sure if there was any colour to them in a different light? The hair around the face and head looked dark brown/black. I only really saw the head peeping round the tree" before I quickly made sense of what was happening and hid. I used to spend every free moment at my Grandparents home in Springwell village, Washington before this happened. And I can remember that night well although I was fairly young at the time.

I had stayed up late watching TV with my grandparents and when I finally did go to bed I was lying in bed and I did not have the curtains closed, there were no houses at the back of us and the house looked out onto greenbelt land. I never had the curtains closed ever that I can remember, I would just watch the sky and the stars till I nodded off. This night I was just lying there in my bed and I moved around a little to get comfy and I lay down on my back with my head to one side looking out of the window. I was just daydreaming and looking outside thinking and all I could see was the conifer trees my Grandfather had planted a few years before. As I lay looking out the window I noticed two eyes looking at me, right away I was scared then as my eyes adjusted to the surrounding trees I noticed what looked like a Gorilla's face peeking through the trees watching me.

Being gripped by Fear I hid under my blanket until I fell asleep, as I said the face kinda just looked like a Gorilla with not much hair on the face at all, it had a short stubby nose, two massive eyes that looked black. The hair around the face and head looked dark brown/black. I only really saw the head of this thing clearly not the body before I hid. But this wasn't the only strange thing that happened.

The second account happened about 10 years after I had seen the Gorilla face and now I was about 22 yrs old. My grandparents had moved not too far away a couple of years before but they were still in the same area just a different house. They moved to Windy Nook in Felling Washington NE. I was sleeping over to look after my Nana due to my Grandfather being in hospital and she didn't want to stay in the house alone. I had a fold out bed to sleep on which was in the sitting room and I would set up the bed in the middle of the floor when I was going to sleep there for the night and that's what I did on this particular night.

I always sleep with the window open because I have trouble sleeping with out background sound and I still never shut the curtains, I was fast asleep and I awoke in the middle of the night at around 2 or 3 am to what I can only describe as a woman screaming like she was being murdered. I mean it made the hair on my neck stand up. It was so bad, and then it stopped just like that and I never heard it again. Nobody reported an attack and none of the neighbours mentioned anything. I looked up different animal calls and sounds like foxes, deer and badgers trying to explain the sound and could not find anything similar. It doesn't match any native sounds I can think of. So I don't know what made this noise or if it's connected to the "Gorilla" from 10 yrs before"?

A Chimp Like Face At The Window. Sevenoaks Sightings 1978 and 1987 - Witness Report: J. Smith October 1978: *"Back when I was a child I lived in Sevenoaks, Kent in a street with a series of houses which was laid out in an oval. The street itself has around 40 houses or so and then fields to the left and countryside, greenbelt and woodland run for a few miles at the back. The countryside was pretty thick in places with pine forests and then oaks and birches, it was quite diverse.*

So I guess you could say I was on the edge of town. I was 10 at the time and it was a Sunday night and I was waiting to watch "How the West was won" with the family. It was a pretty cloudy and foggy and a still night that I can remember. I went to my kitchen to make a cup of tea and in our house we didn't have double glazing at the time, it was a one sheet glass window pane with metal partitions so when we had to cook or boil a kettle and it was cold the condensation would occur quickly and settle on the glass.

I waited in the kitchen for the kettle to boil and out of the corner of my eye I noticed a face appeared in the bottom pane of the window. At first I thought it was just my reflection and then I looked again closely. This time the face pressed itself hard against the window. It was a sort of "chimp and human style face" This "creature" was youngish I would say. I pretended I didn't see it and that would make the event not real, but I was absolutely terrified. I left the room quickly and sat motionless, I couldn't say a word so I decided at the time to draw it, and did so straight away. As an addition to this description I must add the face resembled that of a chimp, with short snout, black/brown eyes but with human type hair everywhere.

Many years later I was to see something very similar at night when out with friends. The second encounter happened in my late teens early twenties around 1987 or so, we used to go to this hill called One Tree Hill after the pub was shut to have a BBQ and drink beers into the early hours. Now One Tree Hill is on top of a rocky ridge. It's kind of strange in that there is this one tree that has a bench beside it and for 200 yards or so it's clear right to the ridge with a 30 yard width of shrub on either side with thick scrub and trees all around.

On this night in particular which was clear but a little cold my friend and I arrived ahead of the other party to start a fire. We parked the car and made our way to the bench which was about a 5 minute walk or so. My friend started gathering wood from the left side and I started gathering from the right. About 10 minutes in I heard a deep, very deep growl,

I dismissed it as Cows or Sheep making noise from the valley below. But then a couple of minutes later I heard it again this time deeper and much more defined, whatever it was growling was on my side and coming my way. The growling noise had real depth to it, that gave the impression that whatever was making it was of a significant size. I placed my firewood on the fire and at the same time my friend joined me. Just as we did so the Grunt sounded again, this time it was a matter of yards away and very loud. I looked at my friend. My friend looked at me and we both said "RUN!" As I ran I looked back and caught a glimpse of a bipedal figure illuminated from the treeline and it was huge.

Now the next day less than 1 and a half miles from the area a lorry driver driving through a remote road said he had nearly hit an "Orangutan" at 6:30am in the morning. The Driver stated that it was "orangey red" in colour. This made the local newspapers that same week. I just stayed silent and didn't tell anyone.

The Henfield Humanoid Thing (Did He Throw A Squirrel At Us?)
1990 - Witness Report: *"It was September 1990 and I was around 16 years old. It was the 40th birthday party of the Mother of my best friend. The family were caravaners who camped often and had obtained use of a field behind a pub to put up tents, caravans, BBQ etc for the weekend. The pub has quite a large beer garden so the field would have been quite a way behind the pub, very near to the River Adur.*

My parents were also attending the party and were along for the trip but I was actually staying the night with my friend in an awning attached to her parents' caravan. I will admit we did consume some alcohol (underage obviously!) earlier on in the evening but it was lemonade mostly and by the time the incident happened I was completely sober. I have an exceptional memory for silly small details and can remember the evening very well, even down to the white cut off jeans I was wearing that were from Gap in Brighton and also a flowery shirt that I got caught on some brambles in a ditch and ripped the back open. After my friend and I had settled down for the night - giggling and talking as girlies do - we heard some commotion outside of the awning. We heard a few twigs and things falling down on the canvas tent roof. It was a bit scary as it was very late and very dark.

We then heard an animalistic growling sort of noise and a large thump and sort of squeak. It sounded like a small animal being thrown at the roof and immediately afterwards (bare with me on this one) I thought of that episode of Blackadder the Third with Amy the female highwayman-type who hates squirrels and shoots one out of a tree and it squeaks as it falls. I even joked and said to my friend 'that sounded like a squirrel hitting the roof'. When I looked outside I saw "someone/something" standing up a tree with its arms above its head.

It was very dark and very broad with a "humanoid shape" and I could just see one continual colour of darkness ie: I couldn't see clothing, no visible eyes or facial features etc, just the outline of a broad shouldered "human shaped thing" up a tree. I am short sighted though so I would not have been able to see detail like hair. I just remember it being very dark in colour and it emitted a sort of guttural sound that sounded like 'wer' (to rhyme with 'her').

There were other people camping in the field and it could have been someone maybe playing a joke but it really didn't look like a 'normal person' to me. I was terrified and immediately stuck my head back into the awning. When I eventually grabbed my glasses so that I could have a proper look, it was gone. I didn't hear it get down and go.

For me to be able to see it without my glasses must have meant it was pretty big and relatively near, but distance is not my forte, I am afraid! My friend asked what it was but this is where my memory fails me (which is unusual for me) as I cannot remember whether she looked out too or just relied on my description. I think we just both went to sleep thinking we were dreaming but when we woke the next morning we both remembered it.

We still talk about it from time to time and she often says "do you remember when that funny thing threw a squirrel at the roof at my Mum's? It's something I thought about often as the years have gone on, and to be honest until I saw your website I didn't realise other people had seen "them too. I just wish I had gotten a better look at "It's" face, but maybe to a young girl it was a blessing in disguise that I couldn't".

I received a report from a couple staying in a caravan who came face to face with a strange creature peeking into the window of the caravan one dark night.

Hassocks Hairy Face At The Window, May 2017 - Witness Report. S. T: *"I want to share with you an experience I had in May this year (2017) while I was holidaying in Brighton, but we were sleeping in our caravan in Coleman's Caravan Park in the Hassocks area. Everything went well and on Tuesday, which was the second night of our holiday we had decided to have an early night, we went to bed and had been settled down for about a half hour when I heard this strange ruffling sound outside the caravan. The campground is quite small and private and we were sleeping with the curtains open. When I opened my eyes to see what was making the noise I got a shock, as I looked to the window and I saw this "thing" looking into the van at us. "It" was not doing anything other than looking at us, "It" was just standing there looking in and watching us in bed.*

It shocked me so much I turned and I woke up my husband. I would describe what I saw as pretty tall. Its head reached the top of the caravan window. The face was pressed up against the glass and the figure was hairy. My husband sat up and lit his lighter and for a brief few seconds we got a good clear look at "It" "It's" shoulders were broad and "his" face was really ugly. "It" had a full beard but with thin hair on top of its head and "It" was showing "It's" teeth. The teeth well they were not like ours they more like dog's teeth. I was so scared. Luckily as soon as my Husband lit the lighter and illuminated the "thing" "It" ran off. I was trying to reason what? Or who? It could've been, I don't know if "It" was just someone homeless living out there but it just didn't seem human like to me. It looked like half an animal."

Plas Dol Y Moch Giant Ape Creature, 1966 - Witness Report. R. Moore: "*I would like to report something that happened to me at the Play Dol Y Moch Outward Bound Centre as a child It would have been about April/ May 1966 the weather was perfect not too cold not quite Summer, I was 13 and It was my school's turn for the third year to have Plas Dol Y Moch Outward Bound Centre for a week it had been gifted to Coventry Council by an old widow for disadvantaged kids to allow them to experience the wilds of the countryside and is still functioning to this day. We would go canoeing, rock-climbing, abseiling and all that stuff. It was great. Also we were taught Orienteering, finding our way in the dark through woods using a map and compass.*

So this one particular night we were paired up and given instructions on how to use the map and compass to navigate the woods at the back of the Centre (which was a huge Manor House affair) Me and my mate were first to set off through the woods, it didn't take long to get through from one side to the other maybe half an hour at the most. So we come to the path that leads back to the centre down a steep slope, this is when "something" very big came crashing through the trees and bushes to our right, Me and my mate just stopped dead still and looked at "It" "It" was sort of "roaring" as I remember "It" was like a huge black shadow it was moving that fast it was hard to make out what "It" was, but you could tell it was thick and bulky. We just dropped all our maps and stuff and ran like hell back to the centre and told all the staff what had just happened. The funny thing is they believed us straight away and called the Police not once did they show any doubt at what we were telling them especially as my mate described it as a "Giant Ape", the Police questioned us very sympathetically and organised a search,

I don't know what happened to all the kids behind us that were about to follow us through the woods, in fact we never really talked about it, after we reported it strange as it seems. Neither myself or my mate back then had never heard of Bigfoot or any such things but I did have a deep interest in UFOs as I had stood underneath a large golden one when I was about eight or nine.

The previous day we were all taken to a local church to see a Giant Hand Print left in a rock said to have been thrown at the congregation as they left Sunday mass one morning, we all took turns in putting our hands into the print to gauge the size, as I remember it was pretty big, this place took me years to find out the name of the village and church its Maentwrog, Twrog Stone".

Torphins Aberdeen. A Huge Hairy Figure Chases the Car, July 1994 - Witness Report. Pete and George: Both Men were walking through a forestry track in the woods near their home in Torphins Aberdeen. When they were nearing the end of the track Pete said he *"saw a dark figure run from the tree's on the left of them, "It"* ran across the track and disappeared into the tree's on the right side of the track. At first, Pete thought it was just a strange man but the figure left a strange foreboding in Pete. George did not see the figure and was busy telling Pete he was imagining things when a face appeared out of the tree's behind Pete's back looking right at George. George was chilled to the bone as the face he was looking at "*looked human, but was not human.*" It darted away just as quickly, and for some reason George threw a large stone in it's direction. The two friends then left the area feeling somewhat unnerved. But as it was a walk they had to do on a regular basis, they would have to return.

A few weeks later the two friends along with a third man they had brought for added numbers were to have another encounter with the 'creature' as they were driving along the road into Torphins, which is a small town two miles away from their first meeting with the "strange Creature." In the witness's own words:" Suddenly from the side of the road there came this, "great muscular hairy figure" bounding out of the forest started to run behind the car. At one point "It" caught up and ran alongside the vehicle for a short time looking in at them keeping up at ease as the "Creature" was not seemingly out of breath as it approached speeds of up to 35 - mph. "

Pete describes the creature as," *strong and muscular, with red glowing eyes, a thick body covered in hair, and about 6ft to 6ft five inches in height, it was jet black in colour.* " The figure ran after them for several minutes and then stopped abruptly in the middle of the road, leaving the terrified car occupants to carry on their journey into Torphins alone. The same or similar 'creature' has also been reported by a lady who lives in an isolated cottage on the edge of the forest where Pete and George first saw the figure.

She has seen it on two occasions watching her house from the woods, she too describes the red glowing eyes. The only other report that I am aware of is that of a man who caught a fleeting glance through high-powered binoculars as it darted through a forest clearing.

But 1 mile away we have this report sent to the Fortean Times which I think ties the two reports together.

"A friend of mine told a story that happened whilst she was out with friends at the back-end of midnight, driving through the back roads near Banchory a small town near Torphins Aberdeen she and another person saw something cross the road in front of their car, and the only description she could give me was 'a Gorilla.' This is the most level headed person I know (some would say overly skeptical) definitely and usually rubbish's any ideas of a Fortean bent I try to persuade her with. But she sticks to her story to this day".

Hill of Keir Footprints - Reported by David Ewen in the Aberdeenshire Evening Express is an article that states "fresh evidence has been found for an ape-like creature roaming Aberdeenshire" Student Peter Dignan found the large footprints on the Hill of Keir next to a drinking trough. Peter explains: "*I was walking the dog and came across them at a drinking trough. The ground was muddy underneath it. At first I just laughed about the footprints but then I went home to get my camera. The day I actually see something is the day I'll find a new route to walk my dog.*"

Now I Believe Him, Snape Wood, A Family of Bigfoot like

Creatures - Witness Report: *"If you are ever in my neck of the woods (no pun intended) there is a place called Snapewood it is part of the old original Sherwood Forest but due to the industrialisation of the Midlands it has become over time a secluded woodland area separated by at least twenty miles and is fenced off with Deer that roam throughout and is now a Nature Reserve. I used to camp there many years ago as a teenager growing up. We would stay overnight often and would hear screeching, this screeching was not birds or any type of wildlife, our camp was ransacked one night as we lay in our tents zipped up and our food was taken, my friend caught sight of what he described as a "huge hairy man with no clothes on" I never saw the creature at the time but it changed my friends life, he would often tell us over and over again about it over the years, we would jest about it to him, he used to go back over the years on his own and sit for hours and he would come back telling us there was a family of "three the youngest being a child Ape like Creature which ran on its hind legs" We thought he was nuts.*

He took us back there some thirty years later and showed us where they could be seen from, You could see if you sat at the top of a disused railway line embankment overlooking the part of woods where an old clay pond had formed (we were around half a mile away) we sat there all afternoon drinking beers until we heard the same screeching sound we had heard as young teenagers. Even now I am lost for words to describe this "huge chestnut coloured hairy man thing" as "he" emerged from the clearing towards the pond and I just sat and watched it in amazement with two of my mates bathing for over half an hour in the water.

The only thing my mate said was "I told you, I told you but you never believed me" He still frequents the woods in Winter and leaves food down there for "them" He told us he has seen the branches you show in your videos. He says they are waypoint markers and when one passes by they will turn it towards the direction they walk towards so others know which way they have gone. I came across this channel by accident and was stunned when I started watching even now at my age I'm over 50 I find it hard to believe but if I hadn't seen it with my own eyes I would never have believed they exist, but I can categorically state they do.⧉

To be honest with myself and my other friends ragged my mate for over thirty five years, it's just not something I would have believed in, But actually seeing "them" although from a distance there was no disputing what it was. My friend was always adamant from the beginning as to what he witnessed all those years ago and he never let it lie either, he would often sporadically call in to see me in passing my house which is adjacent to the woods and he'd tell me that he had been back to the woods with food. I cannot tell you how many times I rolled my eyes and laughed at him. But after seeing it for myself the whole saga was pretty emotional, there was an old wives tale that circulated around the estate and told to young children who stayed out longer than they should have that if you went into the woods at night you would never be seen again.

I'm not sure if it was related to what I saw or if other people have seen "them" down there but it all added to the mystery. There are people that frequent SnapeWood with cameras and clipboards at certain intervals throughout the year but I'm not sure if that's related either as it is a nature reserve. The canopy of the trees is extremely dense and even on the brightest of days it looks dark in there. All I can tell you is I know what I saw that day from the railway embankment and even now it blows my mind just thinking about it".

Sherwood Forest The Strange Father and Son Wildmen, 2013 - Witness Report. Kerry: This is one of the first accounts I took when I joined the early British Bigfoot Research Team with Adam Bird. Back then the accounts were so rare we had hardly any new ones coming in, they were very far and few between, it does show just how far things have moved in the last six years alone. When this was added to the map there were no sighting accounts at Sherwood Forest and now there are two more in that very small area.

"I wish to report something that I saw when I was driving close to Nottingham a few nights ago. I know you don't have Sherwood Forest on your web page but I didn't know who else to contact really, there isn't anyone else I feel I can speak to or who would believe me. I am a normal everyday Woman and I travel this road often and I saw something that I can not quite believe or explain.

I was heading home to Cuckney from work and I was driving along the Worksop Road. It was still light about 4:50pm and I saw two "figures" standing to the side of the road you use as you drive through the forest, "they" were standing just within the trees line. I am going to be honest and say their appearance really scared and unsettled me. They were really tall and also naked and looked like "Cavemen" of some kind? The "big one" stood about 6 1/2 ft tall and was clearly a male. I could see his sexual parts. This male was covered in hair all over, which was brown in colour. "It" had no clothing on it at all. And they both had something strange about their appearance, they had weird shaped heads like a deformed skull, very "Apeish" almost like a "Chimp" but the face looked human too, it's really hard to describe forall they looked like "Apes" they were also very "man" like.

The other smaller one was standing to the side of the larger "Male". The little one was much shorter, only about 3 ft tall and had less hair on its body then the Adult one had. The little one looked the same as the bigger one just younger, it had a deformed head too for a human but still a "human like face within it" I don't know how to explain it to you. It's very hard to put into words what they looked like and how out of place they seemed.

I don't know what I saw that day but it is strange and I have asked myself so many times what "they" were but I don't have an answer. What they looked like to me was a Father and Son or an Adult and Child, haired covered all over, and just standing there using the trees to hide at the side of the road. I wondered if they were just waiting to cross over? But how can these people hide when so many people visit this area?

It just doesn't make sense. They looked for all the world like "wild people" or how you would imagine we once looked centuries ago? I am too scared to tell anyone in case they laugh at me. I can't bring myself to tell anyone else and my husband wasn't keen on me reporting this. But finding out there are other reports makes me feel so much better. I was going to the police but my husband says they will report me to the authorities under mental health act if I do".

Sherwood Forest was once a vast and green land that stretched across the Nottingham area and was frequented of course by Robin and his band of merry men, now chopped into much smaller woods with houses and fields between it would seem a strange place for large hominids to be reported. But if we look at some of the reports found in the smaller woods this huge forest has now become we can still find small little hotspots with reports. Here are just some of them.

A Large Hominid of Loscar Wood, 2014 - Witness Report. R. Lee: *"It was 11.15pm when I was driving home after a day of fishing when I saw something really strange when my headlight lit up an area. I had fished for most of the day and I had packed up my gear and put it all away in the car, I was cold and hungry and ready for home and by now it was just getting on dusk. I was driving along the same road I always use and as I passed Loscar Wood located close to Sherwood Forest and in fact it was once a part of Sherwood Forest. There is a gate there and as I passed it I saw "something" standing next to the gate. It's really hard to explain this but I saw a "huge hair covered figure, just huge, he was not an animal on all fours as he was standing on two legs" I slammed on the brakes as hard as I could and reversed but this hominid looking "creature" (I don't know what else to call it) had gone. No sign of "It" anywhere. I had enough at this point and I put my foot down and got home as quickly as I could."*

The Witness did return some time later with Adam and Paul Bird to do an investigation and an area report at the site. They didn't really feel he could add anymore to the account as it was over very quickly and he was not happy being in the area again. There are other encounters of the wildman very close by. A local teenage myth says that the forest is home to a tall hairy man, whose eyes glow red in the dark. There is a chance that this is a modern version of the tree spirits that were once said to live there in the Forest.

I Almost Hit It With The Bike, Thorpe Perrow Figure, 1983 - Witness Report. A. R: "*I did not know that any UK Bigfoot sites existed until I found yours earlier this week and knew I needed to contact you. You see I had a sighting and experience over 30 yrs ago as a young boy in Yorkshire that I have never been able to explain, I have not told many people over the years and I have only shared it with a trusted few but on seeing the accounts from others you have helped I feel able finally to share it.*

I found the American sites years ago trying to match what I had seen all those years ago and what I saw was so like the American Bigfoot reports that i've been trying to find other UK witnesses ever since, even as far back as the early 80's so on finding you I realised I was not the only one who had seen "It" When I saw the Map of UK Sightings I knew I had to contact you to share the details.

Back in 1983 I lived in a rural area just outside Bedale called Thorp Perrow, the area is pretty rural sandwiched between two National Parks and ample Nature Reserves and country parks with small country lanes, bike paths, many woods and fields and the River Swale, the River Ure and the River Ouse close by it was a good place to grow up as a child.

One year I was around 15 yrs old and Ii was riding my Bicycle back home from the school disco I had just been to. This was at night and with no lights on my bike or the path I was taking it was a little daunting to say the least. I was in a good mood but a little spooked due to the time of night and being alone, so I was singing away to myself outloud to keep my spirits up as it was pretty dark on that land and no one was around. I should say I was riding through the farmland track that leads into the forest as there was a path that made a shortcut home through there for me.

I was peddling away trying to close the distance to home as quickly as I could, singing away and thinking of nothing in particular when Bamm I almost hit "someone" standing on the road, I swerved at the last moment to avoid hitting "them" full on and braked hard. Halting I looked back to see a huge "person shaped thing" with its arms above "It's" head and "It" started to growl/howl/screech at me, "It" was no person and "It" was large and holding "Its" hands up in an angry gesture and making a horrible noise, I'm sorry to say I was terrified, I almost messed my self in fear, all I can remember is the size of this "thing" much bigger than human size, "It" stands out as "large and bulking" now when I think back, the growl was horrible and "It's" eyes stood out the most to me and my attention was fixed on them, those eyes have stayed with me for over 30 yrs.

Looking back all I recall was the initial shock of almost hitting 'someone' in the dark, and then the realisation as I drew to a halt and turned back it was no "person" the mass of "It" was too large to be a person too, "It" was huge and I remember the whites of "Its" eyes and the "inhuman" growl/howl a kind of guttural noise that "It" made at me. I rode off faster than before and got home as quickly as I could. I got the impression "It" was angry.

As I say this was over 30 yrs ago now but it is still with me and even though I now live in the town, dark alleys, country lanes and the woods at night still spook me. I hope this helps others to come forward and share their experiences too".

Motor Cross Rider See "Man like Figure" Cross in front of him.
2018 - Witness Report: *"I am writing to you to report an incident that happened a few weeks ago, I am a keen Motorcyclist and I like to ride Motorcross as its my Hobby, I try to get out whenever I can and I had a really strange experience back in September 2018 that I was hoping you could help me with. I had decided to get in an early morning ride and I headed off to Harwood Forest as I love to ride there and they have a trial set out for Motorcross.*

So after I arrived and I had been riding for a short while I saw something really strange. It was at 8am on a Sunday morning in September 2012 so what I was seeing was impossible, but "It" was right in front of me nonetheless and I couldn't confuse "It" with anything else as nothing else looks like this. I was on a Motorcross bike so I wasn't quiet or anything and they made a fair bit of noise. By this time I was on the main track going through Harwood Forest itself and I noticed "something" coming towards me that was all one solid colour. I thought "It" was someone in a Burka or a Ghillie suit at first as there was just one overall colour, no mixes or breaks in the colour as if this "person" had no clothes on at all.

As I thought "It" was a person "It" didn't bother me at that point I just thought "they" were weird and I just planned to go around "them" so I dropped the bike into second gear and sped towards "them" and at this point "they" were about about 250 yards in front of me. By this point "It" had gone into the trees. I stopped where I had seen it. Put the bike against a tree and looked for what it was or where it had gone? No tracks, no flattened grass or anything. Still don't know what or who it was to this day.

I used to go to Harwood every Sunday for a ride around. This morning was no different until I was going up to the main track from the village. I was in high gear to keep the noise of the bike to a minimum. When I got just past half way up the main track I looked up and something human walked from right to left. As I said earlier I honestly thought it was a person in a Burka or Ghillie suit? I thought how strange?

I'm still unsure as to what "It" was as "It" was all the same colour everywhere, a dark brown colour. I didn't see a face or anything. I couldn't make out any details. It moved and looked like a person, but "It" wasn't human. I could see that.

Coltishall Bridge Creature Multiple Sightings - Late one night between 1960 and 1962, two RAF officers were travelling by car (a Mini) back from Norwich to RAF Coltishall. Passing over Coltishall bridge, they turned left into the High Street and were quickly forced into a sudden stop as "*an enormous black dog*" crossed the road from left to right in front of them. "*As it loped across our line of sight it slowly turned its head, to glare directly and disdainfully into our astonished faces, presenting us with a pair of fiery red eyes. It then slowly swung back its head and continued its measured progress onto the cobbles (if my recall of the village is sound) that stretched up to the shops/houses on the far side of the road. As it hit the cobbles it quite literally vanished.*"

Comparable to the build of a Labrador, its back however was level with the roof of the Mini (approx. 1.35m or 53"). "To put it bluntly, it was a perfectly proportioned giant black dog."

The two officers looked at each other in disbelief, then sped off to the air base.

In the early 1950's, a young woman and her future husband were idling on the Coltishall side of the bridge at nightfall. Walking towards them from 'Coltishall Island' (TG268197, a triangle of land with a petrol station on it, at the meeting of three roads) they saw a black dog, so large, that at first the woman thought it was a pony. As it passed them, the dog turned its head towards them, but continued on, and faded away before it reached the other side. Both witnesses were very scared by the encounter, but managed to cross the bridge themselves soon afterward. The woman still thinks of the incident with fear every time she has to use the bridge.

Mr. Robert Norgate and Miss Agnes Abel of Horstead swear that Shuck passed them one evening on Coltishall Bridge. Both heard pattering feet and heavy breathing. Both looked sharply to see what was there.

Another account [from the 1933 BBC radio programme 'The Dark Shore'] came from a middle-aged couple from Coltishall, who after a stroll on a fine summer evening had stopped on Coltishall Bridge. The man was just striking a match to light his wife's cigarette when Black Shuck 'as big as a calf and as noiseless as death' passed by within a foot of them.

Cantern Brook Woods Grey Hairy Thing, 1980's - Witness Report. D. B: *"I was contacted by a witness from the Cantern Brook area of Shropshire, who lived there as a small child, he explained "as children, we would all play in the woods close to home and on a number of occasions my friends (at least 5 that I can recall) were frightened away while cutting and collecting wood to build dens or ramps, each of my friends described the same "creature." "A huge grey figure" appeared and chased them screaming to the edge of the woods and stood watching them from the edge of the trees."*

They are very old woods with the remains of a Saxon mill and large Oak trees, the stream is some 20m down a steep drop. No children will play down there anymore due to local tales like this. To this day locals report this wood as being haunted due to the Howls and Wails that are heard here and dogs don't seem to like this area at all".

Hairy Teeth North West England, 1972 - Witness Report. P. L: *"I began to wonder about an incident that occurred many years ago when I was a boy. I'm fifty-seven years-old now and enjoy walking in the nearby countryside -just as I did when I was younger. It was 1972 when what I'm about to relate happened and I was twelve at the time. My home town was in the North-East of England. I was out doing something that I and my friends would do most evenings and weekends, as children all across the North would do on light nights, and any chance they had to spend some time outside in the fresh air was taken, hail rain or snow.*

If memory serves, the incident happened one September evening around 9.00 pm. I lived in a small area that is village-like, but it's actually known as the edge of a North-Eastern town and just a couple of hundred yards away from my home, the countryside begins, lots of green belt land, woods and with a few water sources, farmland, the main railway line that connects the South to the North is very close by, along with a large golf course and a River that is only thirty minutes walking away. More housing developments have taken place recently and sadly, the countryside is slowly moving further away.

But on that September night of '72, my three friends and I were playing with a football in one of the streets. The weather was cold and if it had rained that day, I can't recall. But when the incident occurred it was just a cold, damp autumn night. This particular street might seem odd to many as it comprised a road that could accommodate two cars passing each other, a pavement on only one side and the street was contained by a collection of semi-detached houses on the side of the pavement and a row of terraced houses on the other. All the homes had small front gardens bordered by waist-high brick walls or privet hedges of a similar height.

As a side-note, my Father lived on this street as a boy and told me that where the semi-detached houses now stood, was the beginning of the countryside. Like many towns, it just expanded after the Second World War. It was dark on the street that night and the only illumination came from an old-fashioned gas lamp that was situated at the bottom of the street. This was a long time ago and some of the homes still lit their rooms with interior gaslights! So with that in mind, one can appreciate that vehicles were not as plentiful as now and what we were up to would not be disturbed by passing cars.

We were playing a game named 'Kerby' played across the UK no doubt, which involves attempting to hit the corner of the pavement kerb with the ball to score points. One of my friends, an older boy called Kevin -who sadly died a few years ago, kicked the ball in the right direction, but it bounced awkwardly and flew off over the privet hedge into an elderly couple's garden! Being the culprit who'd lost the ball "street rules" apply and he was the one who had to retrieve it, Kevin opened the gate quietly and stepped into the garden behind the chest-high hedge. Then disappeared!

We waited and assumed he was just messing about as we thought we heard grunts or sounds that made me think that the ball was stuck in a bush or something. It must have only been about thirty seconds later when we finally gave up and went into the garden to see where Kevin was. There on his back in the shadows of the hedge, Kevin laid moaning. He looked terrified and as we reached for him, he said "I've just been beaten up!"

Of course, we looked around to see who else could be hiding in the dark garden, but there were no bushes, nothing. Just a dark night in a shadowed garden. The garden consisted of dug-over soil of around twelve feet long by seven feet wide. A high wooden fence separated all the gardens from each other and the privet hedge bordered it from the street. The only other exit apart from the gate that we'd come through, was where the path went up beside the house to connect with a rear garden. From there you could access the open expanse that was partitioned off from other rear-facing houses by tall trees that paralleled the route of the street we were playing in. And we'd seen nobody else come or go. The owners of the house had their curtains closed and I doubt either of the elderly couple had hidden there for half-an-hour or so, when we first began to play our game.

Kevin looked dishevelled, he told us he hadn't been punched or kicked, just 'manhandled' sort of pushed out of the way by the "stranger" that had been hiding behind the privet hedge. When asked what 'he' looked like -because one always assumes it is a male in these situations, Kevin's answer was alarming. He looked at us and said "He had hairy teeth' and that was the total in his description. We can assume whoever this person was had arms and legs, due to his-or-her's ability to 'manhandle' our friend and also flee from the scene. Being a couple of years older than myself and the others, we didn't press him further and I can state that I knew Kevin all of his life and he was far from having an overeager imagination. He clammed up and we didn't push the matter or ask him any questions. Just like kids all over the world, a few minutes later we were back playing our game and all was forgotten about this weird encounter with 'the man with hairy teeth.'

A few years later, I was sitting in a local Pub with Kevin and jokingly brought up that incident of our youth and I was surprised at the serious look on his face. He assured me that it did happen and considering he actually still lived in the area -now being an adult and a parent had forced him to analyse the short-lived encounter in the gloom of that hedge.

Although this time he did go into more detail and explain what he saw when he went over the hedge that night. He didn't see any eyes and added that it really annoyed him because one can tell a lot from someone's eyes, he said. He couldn't say he felt clothes during the tussle, nor if the "stranger" smelled strange in any way, although being in a dark, dank place under a hedge may confuse any conclusion!

The only thing he kept saying was that he saw "hairy teeth" and when asked to describe these 'teeth' he struggled and just said he knew there was "hair and teeth" and that is all he would say. I suggested that whoever had obstructed him from retrieving the football may have had a beard, but he just shrugged and said he didn't know.

Time moves on.

Living in another area of the town not too far from where the above incident occurred, my Wife and I took a walk along a country lane that would bring us out back on my 'old stomping ground' This was around 2010 and we were getting to the age where retirement was on the cards and some might say that memories become really important!

I had heard that Kevin had passed away a few years before and after chatting to his widow at her front-gate for a while, we carried on our way. We spoke to a couple of people that I had grown up with and we came across a family that we also knew we began talking about 'the old days' and how things used to be. But, I was surprised when my friend's wife answered an indifferent question about how things were now that the area was busier with traffic and such.

She remarked gruffly that "the kids were still up to their usual pranks and from time to time, playthings, vegetables and shrubs would disappear from the gardens in the area Her husband agreed and added that his allotment-garden had taken a few hits from someone he suspected was after sabotaging his prize vegetables."

But when one of her children, a small boy of around eight or nine chimed in and said "it wasn't the kids -but that Man with hairy teeth, the lad grabbed my focus. But not wanting to raise any alarm-bells and make a big-deal of the boy's comment, I looked quizzically at his mother and casually asked what he meant. She explained that for a few years now, when the kids in the area had been coming in from their wanderings in the countryside or if they'd arrived home late from doing whatever kids get up to in the evenings, they'd occasionally mention that they'd seen the Man with hairy teeth!

Was or is it an unshaven transient that has quietly gone about for over forty years nightly-visiting the gardens of a small community or is it one of your guys? Something we just don't fully understand yet"?

The Penn The Crouching Wildman, 2000's - Witness Report: The witness who was around 15/16 at the time of his sightings was hunting in fields in the Penn Area of Wolverhampton with his friend. He was in his usual position within the field and had his rabbit gun and a torch light to light up the field, but as he was scanning the light across the area, the torch picked up a crouching human type figure, much bigger than an average human and in his own words "*it was huge in height and width*" his friend promptly ran off leaving the witness alone, so he followed suit and legged it also. he is older now but he is still certain of what he saw that night and said "*it was not of the normal world.*"

Another Sighting In Penn. Wolverhampton Wildman Or A British Bigfoot? May 2018 - Witness Report: *"I'm really unsure what I saw and I don't know enough about any of this to hazard a guess, I know what it wasn't. But I'm unsure as to what "It" was. "Well I guess you can help me decide that after I tell you what I saw, it happened in early May 2018 I was running late for work so I decided to take a short cut through the country lanes towards Kinver to pick up the A449 further down. I was down the back end of Lower Penn by Wolverhampton on a single track road called Showell Lane, it's a single track road with woods and fields to both sides, as you come to the bottom of the road there's few houses and an old very overgrown public footpath, a right of access or something that's set back about 50ft from the road, and it was when I got here I saw what I first thought was a man in a hunting suit or a sniper's suit thing with all the shaggy hairy stuff you see them with, but this was orangy in colour like a red setter dog but lighter.*

I kept looking and it was then I noticed the sheer size and bulk of this "thing" and I knew it couldn't be what I initially thought "It" was, because this thing I reckon it was at least 7 ft tall and was massively thick around the chest and shoulders like an American footballer with all the pads on! I was quite a bit away from it and it was sort of stepping back into the shade of the foliage but it was scary even so, and I'm a man of 6 ft and 22 st who's trained for many years but I felt scared and floored it Which I now regret! I've since after doing a bit of research found quite a few sightings around the Midlands and Shropshire areas and now my fear has turned more into a need to understand what I saw that morning."

The Black Country Stalker, Autumn 2018 - Witness Report. H. S:

"On Tuesday morning I was up on Baggeridge Ridge at around 9.30 when I saw a elderly gent walking his dog. He said morning to me and carried on down towards the car park. I finished around 10 and headed for the cafe. The gent I had seen walking his dog was in there too. I got a coffee and sat down and after a short while he came over and sat down at my table. He pointed at my t-shirt (Gone Squatchin') and asked If I believed in it. I said yes and told him that I investigate the sightings here in the UK. He said he had something to tell me but wanted his wife present when he did so we arranged to meet back at the cafe on Thursday at 9am.

Thursday I got there around 8.55 am and the couple came in together at around 9.15 am. We sat for a short time and had coffee and we chatted in general. I brought up the subject of bigfoot sightings and the old fella said not here and nodded for us to leave and we left the cafe at that point. They led me up a path that I know well as I had put owl boxes up there about 10 months previously. This area is one I call horseshoe path because it follows the treeline in a half circle. The path is only single file wide with trees on both sides of it. One side falls down hill and the other side has a slight incline and it is very quiet there. Very few people use it as it's mostly off the beaten path. We reached an area halfway around the trail where we stopped and then they told me what they had seen earlier.

One morning around 9.30 am in April 2017 the elderly couple were out walking their little dog as they did most mornings. They chose this path as their dog does not get on well with other dogs and it's very rare to see anyone else walking up there. As they walked along the man noticed a dark figure moving in the trees around 30 feet away. He thought it was strange as whatever "It" was "It" seemed to be watching them from behind a tree then ducking every time "It" was noticed. The man decided not to say anything to his wife as he did not want to alarm her in any way. They both continued to walk slowly with the dog but the figure stayed around the same pace they were and continued to try and remain hidden whilst keeping pace with them from behind the trees.

After around 10 minutes had passed the man's wife noticed he seemed anxious and asked him what the matter was. He told her what he had noticed and pointed the figure out to her. At first she could not make anything out in the trees but eventually she spotted "It" and saw "It" duck back in and start peeping at them from around the tree it was hiding behind. The dog then started barking and growling at "It." They rushed as best they could with the dog now on the lead and eventually reached a fork in the path and they knew that one way would take them back to the car park. As they turned at the bottom of the path that leads out of the woods and onto open fields they stopped to catch their breath. As they looked back from where they had come from, the "creature" had stepped out onto the open path. They both agreed it stood upright, was very dark in colour and covered in hair. She said "It" was around 8 feet tall, but he said "It" was closer to 7ft. "It" didn't try to follow them any further.

They got back to their car and now they don't walk in that area any more. In fact they rarely use Baggeridge Country Park anymore, so our accidental meeting was a spot of good fortune. They wish to remain anonymous, but I have no reason to disbelieve their story as they seemed very scared to me and the elderly lady had to keep wiping tears from her eyes".

The HunchBack Of Park Lime Pits, 1980's - Witness Report: "*Hi Deborah. I've been watching your recent video concerning the Woodmill Hairy thing and it has jogged a memory I had from my childhood. I grew up in the village of Rushall just outside Walsall which has quite a lot of greenbelt fields and woodland. I used to love walking in a particular area called Park Lime pits which was a lime quarry but is now a Nature Reserve, the quarry has now been filled with water and stocked with plenty of fish. Around 40 years ago children would go and play in the woods there -alas children had more freedom then. One girl in my class told me about something that happened to her Brother and his friend when they had stayed out longer than they should have, and it was getting dark when they came across what they described as a hunch backed man walking along the railway embankment.*

They described the "figure" as raggy, dirty and unkempt and they could hear that he was breathing heavily. She said her Brother and his friend ran away and were genuinely very frightened when they got home. I told my friend and one evening as children do, we actually went looking for the hunchbacked Figure they had seen!

Of course we never found anything so just dismissed it as fantasy. I'm wondering now though that perhaps there was something to it and the boys may have seen a "wild man" The area has food sources and water, a canal, there are mine shafts and workings and even a golf course not too far away. Further along the railway line down Bosty Lane there is also a patch of woodland called Linley Wood. It may have also been quarried at one time as the land undulates and is cavernous in some parts. I roamed all over the place when I was a kid but we never ventured in that wood. I just never felt comfortable there. I'm not in contact anymore with the girl who told me this tale so unfortunately can't verify the story. It's still intriguing, though I thought I'd pass it on".

Troglodyte In The Bushes and Brambles - Witness Report. S.H: *"A long time ago now back in the late 70's early 80's I was going out with a girl who lived not too far away, her brother and I were pretty close and we would walk the dogs sometimes and have a chat while we did so. Back then we were in the Hayes Heath area walking along the canal there, when the dogs we were walking started to act up, we were beside some thick bramble bushes not the sort of thing you would expect someone to hide in, but that's exactly how the dog was reacting. I had a large torch with me and I pointed it towards the bush and hit the ON switch, it switched on fine but every time I pointed it at that bush the torch would go out.*

It really spooked us after a while so we started to walk off down the path trying not to look back, but after a while I did look back and saw the weirdest thing, where the bushes were there was now a strange "Troglodyte" looking thing just standing there watching us. It had a really strange glow to it, almost as if it was emitting "Its" own light somehow. We just left but I have never forgotten the event."

Large Hairy Man Sitting In The Woods, Just Watching Me? 1998 - Witness Report: *"I have re-thought of an incident that occurred several years ago on the edge of Dartmoor and I think it may be of some interest to you. I have never really been able to make much sense of it but thought you may be able too. I'm writing this account around 12 years after it occurred, however I can* remember it quite clearly, I think it was around 1998 – 1999, I was staying at the Haldon Lodge caravan site near Kenford in Devon.

I have spent a great deal of time in the Haldon hills, especially around the Bird of Prey watching point and the surrounding pine woods. On one occasion while alone I explored a really dense area of pine trees, literally moving on hands and knees to get through the area. I was heading for a clearing on the hill side that was visible from the caravan park.

After maybe half an hour or more I came across a huge clearing surrounded by trees. It was in this area that I encountered something that I could not really work out. Shortly after emerging from the tree line I immediately spotted what looked like a large hairy human shape sitting on a tree stump. But this figure was huge at first I thought it looked like a "scruffy man in a fur coat" which puzzled me however as it was a blistering hot day. Who would wear a fur coat in this heat and tromp for an hour to sit on a stump? Could it be some old tramp or hermit type?

Whatever "It" was "he" sitting there, I believe I was seeing "It" from behind. And I thought "It" was a person at first, so although I was a little on edge I decided to move a little closer to see if "It" was just a stump or a trick of the eye. In doing so I noticed what looked like the back of a head although only the top, again this appeared to be hairy and connected to the main body which was also hairy and I noted that the hair colour was a brown/grey colour. I could not tell if it was fur or hair but could now get a good gauge of its size.

Whatever "It" was "It" was big, easily the size of a very large man and very wide. It was at this point that I took one step closer and what I presumed was the back of the head moved down and slightly to the side as if moving around to look at me. Did "It" know I was there all along? It was at this point I had had enough and moved back towards the trees slowly and quietly, when I looked back whatever "It" was "It" had now changed position and appeared to be looking straight in my direction. Once in the trees I ran as quick as I could towards the road. As I have already noted the clearing was really hard to get to, it took me a great deal of time to reach it and that spot is surrounded by dense trees on all sides, so I was at a loss as to what this was. I can't really see this as a "man in a costume" or a "tramp or wild person" as this was not an area people visit and again it was very hot.

I re-visited the area several years later and located the tree stump in question. It was apparently clear by now that whatever "It" was "It" was huge. When working out the distance between where I was standing and the size of the stump, "It" was Clearly very big, much bigger than an average sized male".

A Wild Man Sitting In The Wood Eating - Leigh Woods, Somerset, August 17th 2015 - Witness Report. Harry: According to one local newspaper a Bristol resident says he witnessed an ape-like creature as it ate a piece of food with what he believes may have been improvised eating utensils. 58-year-old Harry, a retired man in Somerset said that he was walking through the Leigh Woods Nature Reserve on August 17 2015 when the strange event took place. *"I usually take my dog, but lately I have avoided taking her there because she has been getting very skittish for some unknown reason".*

As I was walking along I suddenly began hearing noises as if someone was "snapping twigs" and "making squeaky sounds". "I thought it may have been a deer off in the brush, so I went off the path to look,". "This is when I saw this strange "ape creature" "It" was sitting in the brambles, digging in the earth with a twig." "It" did this for about 5 minutes, then picked something up and began eating it. Harry believes this was a piece of raw meat.

"Then "It" took another twig and used it to pick pieces of meat from between "Its" teeth." But Harry was also aware that the strange-looking being appeared to be "communicating with something". "It" kept looking left and was talking to something off in the trees that I couldn't see, and I thought I heard movement from where "It" kept looking. When I say talk, it was more like "It" grunted and squeaked,"at one point "It" started doing something with the twigs, crossing them over on top of each other, like "It" was weaving something. All in all, I watched this "thing" for 25 minutes. It was only when "It" stood up and walked off that I got up and left. When "it" stood, it grabbed a large tree branch and snapped it off quite easily, and then leaned it against another tree. Then it walked off and I never saw it again."

Harry says he was about 200 yards away and managed to discern the physical features of the "creature" "When"It" stood up I'd say "It" was about 6 feet tall. "It" was old looking and "It" had a grey skin. I could see that "It" had human features, but "It's" face looked more ape-like with a broader nose and cheeks, and a jaw that jutted out and looked like"It" was curved. "It" looked like a prehistoric man from "Land That Time Forgot", the old Doug McClure film. "It" was covered in grey hair, which had black streaks in it. "Mostly grey though," said Harry, also adding that "it" also had what appeared to be "small breasts" but that "It" looked like a male because there was "something" in the crotch area.

The man explains that even though he was confused about what he was witnessing, he is sure that "It" wasn't an animal. "It" wasn't a horse or dog or anything like this. "It" was like an ape man. It was like a man living wild - like a Neanderthal or something similar. I have heard of Bigfoot, but "It" wasn't like one of those, like the giant wrestler type of thing. I searched for Bigfoots in the UK and came across your articles on these sightings so I thought I would share this with you." Harry claims he was not "scared or worried" because the creature "seemed friendly" although, he adds, it didn't get a chance to see him.

Quote from the Bristol Post: 'Leigh Woods has had a reputation for being haunted for some time. Years ago, tramps lived in the woods favouring the Abbots Leigh end and avoiding the Leigh Woods part because of it's evil reputation. It was said that loud screams could be heard in the night".'

The Carmyllie Bigfoot/s, 1981/82 - Witness Report. Charmaine Fraser: "These experiences happened at my grandparents' property and they lived out in the Carmyllie Forest and we spent a lot of our childhood there as children, staying over at the farm house, it was very heavily wooded back then and there is a quarry and steams, my Brother currently lives there.

The first incident took place during the day when I was sent out to get the newspapers that got delivered to the neighbours at the bottom of the road. I was with the dog and we were coming down the long path that leads to the track running past the bottom of the property and out onto the farm road. Just before I got onto the track the dog stopped suddenly and started to growl, whine and bare her teeth.

I remember seeing the hair rising on her back, but I carried on past her for a few paces ending up on the track. I just thought she had heard a fox or something and that had her spooked. I carried on to get the newspapers and I looked up at that moment and I couldn't believe what I was seeing, I saw a "large black figure" further along the track standing with "Its" back to me. I don't think "It" knew I was there or was it just that "It" wasn't bothered by me being there, "It" was reaching up to a branch on a tree, and just carried on as if I wasn't watching.

"It" was at the side of the track and was very tall, and "It" had a thick build with no neck and wide shoulders "It" was also hairy all over. I remember standing in shock for a second or two before screaming and turning to run back to the house, as I screamed "It"slowly started to turn around but I didn't hang about to see "It's" face. Needless to say my reports of seeing a monster were not taken seriously and dismissed as it probably being a neighbour. I can't give an exact year but I was around 8/9 years old (This is an estimation as I remember drawing a picture of it in primary 5 at school) so that puts it around 1980/81 and I don't have an exact time of year but the leaves were out on the trees so it would have been sometime between early summer and Autumn.

There were two further incidents around that time also, but they are more tenuous I feel but I will share them in the hopes *somebody remembers another account like mine. Late one night when we were driving along the empty road, we were coming up the road in the car and just as we were turning right onto the track where I had seen "him" there was a "figure" further up the road, "he" was up the road facing us and "he" was looking towards the headlights of our car. You couldn't see "him" clearly but I briefly made out a "humanoid shape" and there was "orange eye shine" reflecting from the lights, "It" was just standing in the middle of the road looking at us. At the time I told myself "It" was probably a person.*

The final incident was when we were allout picking wild raspberries and we heard something way back in the woods, a long, deep wail. The adults in the group looked at each other and commented on the howl, wondering what it was but then they dismissed it and carried on with what they were doing".

Another Witness To The Carmyllie Bigfoot. Footprints In The Snow, 2012/13 - Witness Report. A. K: *"I would like to report an experience I had a few years ago. I never really told anyone about what happened at the time because as you know talking about bigfoot makes you a crazy person in some people's minds, but I just recently found out that there have been two other sightings near a quarry not far from me just outside of Carmyllie, and I live very near there. It was during the winter of 2012 or 2013, which if you recall was very intense. In Carmyllie, the snow was a foot deep on flat ground, and many feet deep in snow drifts. I was walking the family dog down a dirt track that provided access to a stretch of farm plots. The track stretches between the main roads that run through this area, and a wooded land plot that stretches further South.*

About a little further than half way down the road, I saw what appeared to be an extremely large footprint in the snow. It was slightly softened by snowfall, but was clear enough to make out that it was a bare foot shape rather than a shoe or a boot shaped impression, and the print was maybe 1.5 times the length of my boot. This made it by my judgement a little longer than a foot and a half. Judging by the way the footprint was orientated, it seemed that "whatever" had left it was walking from the field on one side, to the field on the other, it looked like whoever had left the print was cutting sideways across the road.

Considering that the road was at that point maybe 4 foot across due to the snowdrift, and there was only one foot print on it, the "creature" that left it must have been quite large. I tried to see if there were any more footprints around, but I couldn't find any. I think this might have been because the snow that would normally fall on the footprint was being blown into the drifts at either side of the path, so this print was slightly more protected as it was being snowed out less than the other footprints, and thus remained clear while the others were hidden by the falling snow.

As strange as this was, I deemed that it was probably nothing to worry about. It could have been caused by any number of things, so I left it and continued on. Once I reached the wooded area at the end of the road is when the scenario became very intense. For detail, the area also had a lot of low, scrubby bushes. With the snow, these bushes could be about 5 foot tall, coming up to my neck. Once me and the dog got to the wooded area, the dog reacted, she seemed to have seen something before I did and began barking and lunging.

Before I saw the "creature" I heard it. A sort of deep, long "ooooohhh" sound, which caused the dog to stop barking and start squeaking and whining in fright. Finally, just before I was about to turn and leave for the sake of the dog, and frankly for my own sake, I witnessed this great, big "creature" rise from behind one of the bushes. It stood easily 3 heads over the top of the bush, and seemed disproportionally wide at the shoulders and neck, and was almost black in colour. The snow also seemed to glint off its eyes, making them pop out at me slightly more than, say, a regular humans would. While the visibility was slightly damaged by the snow, this creature was only maybe 5 metres in front of me, and it still dwarfed me. It was at this point that the dog took off, and I took off after it. I didn't look back.

Since then, I have tentatively returned to the road, but haven't seen any trace of the creature. I generally don't buy into these sorts of things, but I suppose something like this only needs to happen once to convince you. Regardless, I've never told this story, and am only now revealing it due to my discovery of the other stories. Perhaps there is something in this area that we haven't discovered yet"?

The Black Weir Pond Epping Forest. Two Boys Have a Terrifying Experience, 1974 - Witness Report. C. H: This was reported by a gentleman who had an experience back then with a friend when they were both out fishing in the Blackweir pond area. Known to locals as The Lost Pond or even The Suicide Pond it is an eerie place to be in the daytime, let alone at night with only a pocket knife for protection.

"The Lost Ponds is a strange place at the best of times, I have been to that area so many times as a boy with my friends, we would fish late or just play as boys do, coming home when we were hungry, there was a weird feeling to this place even in the day but this night it got weirder still." The lost pond is in the area of Loughton Camp within Epping Forest, one of the old Hill forts from ancient times.

The proper name for the water source as I mentioned was the Blackweir Pond, but it was known to us locals as the Lost Pond because it is hidden away in the middle of the forest in a hard location to get into and it is not visible to any passers by, there are large trees and bushes all around it, so that's how it got its name but not its reputation. Even the pond itself has an eerie feel. It was a strange circular-ish pond where we used to fish at night for carp. I say strange because it had a local and well told reputation at school as the suicide pond, it always feltl dark and solemn when your there to be honest, and its said normal sane individuals would inexplicably be overcome with grief or sadness and throw themselves into the waters and drown themselves for no reason, well that was the local story at least, but we were not deterred from fishing as it was a good little spot, quiet and out of the way. Not many people fished it other than us so it was always a place we would head too, there and "the gravels" were our two favourite spots.

On one of these fishing trips we had headed to the pond and fished for a while and it had gotten too late in the evening, it would have been back in the mid 1970s, and we had encamped on the bank of the pond, in an area of clear gravel and a little away from the forest (as it's much easier to cast off), we placed the fishing umbrellas behind us to form a wind break and preserve some warmth as it was getting cold. So we baited and then cast off, the floats were in the water and we sat with our torches shining on them in the hopes of a bob or two. We fished for a couple of hours chatting away about this and that, feeling fine and enjoying ourselves. Not much was happening except for the odd small nibble from crucian carp that the pond held.

We were sitting there in the quiet with just the gentle bob that could be heard and the woods were quiet when from behind us there was a noise and it was coming out of the forest, there came a loud shuffle in the leaves, like a loud Thump or a heavy "Thud!" and then "Thump" "Thud" again, as we listened we heard a really loud extremely heavy thud! Then after a second there was another another "Thump!" and then one after another they seemed to be getting closer to us each time. The next "Thud" was the scariest of all as this time it wasn't leaves we heard but you could hear the sound of gravel being crunched, so whatever "It" had it come out of the forest and was heading toward us getting closer all the time. The steps were about a second and a half apart. "Thud! Thump! Thud!"

As strange as this may sound, it sounded to me at the time as though a very heavy man had "hopped" out of the forest and was hopping towards us. Or something very heavy on two legs unseen was coming our way? We were looking at each other dumbfounded with a mix of fear and annoyance at first that this might be one of the Epping Forest "Perves" that so many tales circulated about and this place is known for old murders and strange ghostly tales, so we grabbed the torches and rod rest as that's all we had really to defend ourselves with except some tiny sheaf knives for cutting the line, so they would have to do as "weapons" and we both stepped out from the umbrellas at the same time in a show of strength to do battle in best Schoolboy tradition. After the count of Three 1, 2, 3 we both jumped at the same time from behind the umbrellas ready to attack. But there was nobody there. Nobody running back to the trees trying to hide, no sign of anyone, just empty space where ever we looked? There was no sign that anybody had been there and no sound from the surrounding forest to indicate that someone was running back that way escaping from us. What could be that heavy and yet vanish that quickly and silently?

We'd had enough at this point, and in absolute terror we packed up quickly (faster than I have ever done so before or since) and ran for it, well, fast walked through the dark forest carrying all our gear. Our torches pointing everywhere - just in case, banksticks and sheath knives at the ready. It was so dark in there you couldn't see what was just up ahead or behind it was terrifying. I still have no idea what could have made the noise we heard, what would "Thud," "Thump" like that, you could feel the "Thud" on the ground and it was so loud. Suffice to say that although this occurred some 30 years ago it remains vivid in my memory even now - because of the complete terror that I felt at the time. I will never get over that night and I no doubt will always remember it and even to this day I can't work out what could have been that heavy to make that much noise, you could feel those thumps on the ground"?

Epping Forest Animal Attacks and Howls, 2014 - Witness Report. G.B: "*I wrote to BBR as I live very close to Epping forest and know* *of horse attacks and missing animals in the area, the neighbours have chatted about it and you hear it every now and again from people who keep horses or use the forest itself. The horses I am talking about were/are still on a farm next to the forest, there is a stables they house the horses and they belong to various people. The stable contacted the Police as over the course of a couple of months 3 or 4 of the horses were as the Police put it "slashed." Now the area they are kept in is not the easiest to get into, there are muddy fields on one side and the other side butts up to the M25 motorway. One of the industrial units down that lane closest to the stables has CCTV and is gated so how would people get into the stable yard unseen and unheard? What if an animal had tried to catch the horse and the wounds were claw marks. I believe the claw marks were around the neck and flanks.*

I'm a very suspicious and security minded person, ie: I see when things are out of place and I like to keep a note of what is happening. And I also watch for things or people out of character moving around the area. You could say due to the animal attacks I'm not leaving anything to chance. One night I heard a howl that I can not explain. The night it happened I was on the sofa just thinking and watching the moon through the patio doors, when I thought I heard a howl that sounded out of place and I couldn't recognise the noise other than to say "a howl" now to anyone else they wouldn't think anything of it but I took note of this weird howl due to the horses being messed with in the forest there.

It may have been a deer calling or a fox or owl or dog but there's only a few dogs around here and they are not out at night and I'm used to all those noises that stood out to me as unusual. There was not any wind and it was not a night that the local club was open.

There were no people around, It was a distinct howl one long one and I judged it to be within a mile of the house. I hunt and do bushcraft so i'm often outdoors alone. We have had cats go missing from around here and no dead carcasses have been found as of yet.

A local paper reported that Irene Dainty encountered a four foot, hairy creature with large feet and animal-like eyes close to her home. The creature ran off and jumped over the wall of the nearby Three Jolly Wheelers public house."

Ashridge Woods Growls and Objects Thrown, July 2015 - Witness Report. G. G: "*I wanted to report something strange that happened when I was walking round Ashridge Woods in Hertfordshire like I always do when some odd things happened which I can't explain, I'm not jumping to conclusions and I have tried to debunk all of this but up to now I have ruled out all legitimate possibilities off what you would normally find in the woods.*

I was walking in there as I often do but on this occasion as I had something small thrown at me from the trees. It didn't fall from above but hit me as if it had been thrown with a purpose, not hard but in the correct direction. I felt like a fir cone and then while I was pondering this I heard a low growling and I just felt like something was watching me, I've felt being watched before in these woods and I have also seen shadows which with the way my eyes are im not worried about but the last times I saw something out of the corner of my it kinda scared me.

There was a tree in the pathway which seemed to have been placed across the track blocking the trail. I couldn't see any marks from the tree being dragged there? no tyre tracks either. I was puzzled when I looked around to find where the tree had been broken to look at the stump. I couldn't find it and as there was nowhere clear to me that the tree had come from I looked the whole area over again. I went back there today and the tree is not there. It has completely gone again, no tyre tracks or dragging marks seen. I'm not really sure what growled at me, or what sent the pine cone. But I will keep visiting to see if anything else happens out there".

Strange Happenings in the Woods, Ambresbury Banks, Epping - Witness Report. C. L. H: "*Ambresbury Banks between the Wake arms Roundabout and Epping is another late Iron Age earthwork in the area of Loughton, where I spent much of my teenage years. The ends of the bank at this point were revetted with coursed pudding stone blocks. Finds at the site have included flints and flint arrowheads and shards of red, grey and black pottery, which suggests a construction date of around 700 BC and occupation until 42 AD. The hill fort today lies in Epping Forest although it is right next to the B1393 Epping to Loughton road. The area within is completely wooded and crossed by a few paths which are supposed to be only for walkers, for Ambresbury Banks is a scheduled monument, but some use them for motorbikes and cycles because they don't care about the past.*

With the above legend in mind this place became a focus of investigations for me in the late 1970s, it encompassed History, legend, archaeology and was close to my home in Loughton. Unfortunately, nothing was ever witnessed there in Boudiccan terms, no women in white dresses, no Briton warriors or Roman Legionaries, or indeed any apparitions at all of any date.

I found the entrance via the rampart near to the Epping road a rather peaceful place, and indeed most of the fort was. But the further one went into the interior and approached the rear, in the areas that fewer people would visit, the stranger the place became. On one of my visits I was convinced that I heard the sounds of footsteps following me so I ducked out of sight and waited to see. This was Epping Forest after all and who knows what could have followed me in there, but when I stopped walking so did the footsteps, and they didn't start again once I set off again.

There was also always a feeling of being watched in this part of the fort, not exactly hostile, but then again not exactly friendly either. This presence has been reported by others walking in this area as well.

One other thing of note perhaps, our dog didn't like the area either, and while usually he would be running free well away from me and running back, here he would keep close by absolutely around the legs almost tripping me up and looking around, he was definitely nervous.

Chris 7/12/17

This is one of the many accounts from this area, and reports come in over the years that I have filed away in the Loughton camp area. Never sure enough to add them to the sightings map but noting a similarity in them with many of the reported Bigfoot Accounts we hear.

These are just some of the notes I had made on the area: There is an old tale from 1313 of a hermit named Kate who lived within a "cellar" in the woods, Reported amongst other things are drumming rhythmic sounds, shadows and people being followed or stalked within the woods. Strange ghostly lights and mists? In 2004 a witness named Lee. A stated "Myself and two friends had been there at the camp one night and the wind began to blow, making the trees creek and whistle as the wind rushed through them. The atmosphere was really edgy and we retreated through the woods back to the car almost immediately. I wonder if anyone has investigated here or knows anything more about the sites."

Another witness also stated. "Hello there, I wasn't sure whether to even enter this post as it all seemed too weird but this is what happened to me at Loughton camp. My friend and I were chilling up at the beginning of the foot of the hill for a while before dusk and spent an hour undisturbed by humans, we were a fair way into the forest and heard nothing but animals. As it got dark we decided to leave, but I had to take a leak first so as I was off doing my thing we both heard a deepish drum banging in a slow rhythm from somewhere in the woods.

I kinda joked about it but we were both a bit freaked, it was getting pretty dark and all. The most odd thing though was the deep groaning we heard as we were walking briskly out of the woods, it seemed very lo-fi and I asked my mate to stop and listen but he was too scared, I wasn't even up there investigating and i was wondering if anyone knows of other experiences there cos I'd like to know if similar things have been witnessed. The drumming was totally bizarre and we heard or saw no one or any unnatural noises other than the two i just described."

Another account on a paranormal thread states: "On one occasion in the 1970's during the day, a friend and myself were at the camp, it was overcast and very little wind was around. We were pelted (as though a strong wind was in force) with Beech nuts. We moved and got the same treatment - then realisation dawned on me we were standing under OAK trees. I kept a beech nut from my Parka's hood for years afterwards."

An Unseen Predator In The Woods. Newmilns Kilmarnock - Witness Report. Martyn: "*I experienced something really weird when I was a kid and I wanted to report it and to see if anyone else has ever experienced the same thing. My family are a traveler family and in my younger days we would move from area to area as we needed too. At one point we moved from a farm in Blackrod which is near to Chorley in Lancashire, we lodged on that farm for a long time while we stayed in one of the caravans but there came a time when the farmer decided to sell up and move and when he did buy his new farm in Scotland we decided to move with him.*

It was a long move as we had to travel out of England and into Scotland and that seemed like a really long way to travel to a kid my age. The area we moved to was called Newmilns and it was in Kilmarnock. It was very remote and we were situated about 10 miles from the nearest town, sometimes in winter we had to literally use a tractor to get food from the nearest village and back because the snow was that deep.

The farm was absolutely huge from my recollection around 2000 acres surrounded by dense forests and not far from us was the moors, rivers and streams and no people around except for us. As a 10yr old lad my Dad used to send me out hunting with a 22 rifle to catch and kill rabbits, pheasant and small birds for the ferrets we kept. And also collecting wood for the log burners in the caravans was another of my responsibilities around the place, so I was often out on my own in the woods and fields.

I have heard some real freaky stuff out in those woods and I have seen a lot of dead animal carcasses that looked out of place even to me being used to the countryside and the way animals take and kill prey, I didn't recognise the "animal" responsible for those kills. When I think back and with what I know now I can say there was a lot of "ufo" activity in that area, we all saw strange lights in the sky at night all the time, so often as a young child it had become the norm. As I said I was only young and only now as I'm older and have access to the internet that I started to put 2 and 2 together so to speak.

What sticks out the most in my memory is one day in particular, I was out hunting as usual about a mile away from where we were camped, I was moving quietly keeping my eyes open and trying not to disturb any birds until I wanted to. And all of a sudden out of nowhere I had an overwhelming sense that someone or something was watching me. I realised everything around me went dead quiet, no bird song, no wind in the trees, nothing! Just dead silence that was very unnerving.

I was overwhelmed by fear and looking all around me trying to make out someone hiding in the shrub and movement of sound that would give them away. It wasn't the middle of the night and dark, it was day time and the light shimmering through trees can play tricks on the human mind. As I was looking I thought I saw something moving in there but it's so dense in those pine trees and I just realised "they" could be anywhere so I set off running.

Whatever was in there was following me out of the woods crashing and banging but every time I looked back and I could not see it. I ran really fast as a kid. I was quite proud of the fact that nobody could catch me at running back then, but whatever it was, it was keeping up with me and I think catching up to me also. I heard branches and twigs snapping behind me but at that point I stopped looking back because I knew "It" was hot on my heels. I hear of all these missing 411 cases now and all that runs through my mind is "I could have been on that list but I out ran it."

The Kits Coty, Giant Hairy Man Ape 1940's - Witness Report: "I was contacted by a YouTube viewer who was watching a video on an account I had released in 2017 on The Medway Area of Kent, the video triggered a memory told by a Mother who had a school friend when much younger who had witnessed a similar hairy creature which she called The Giant Hairy Ape Man: I remember my Mother telling me this story about a school outing where a young girl saw something very strange that scared her, so when I heard your accounts online from other people who lived around The Medway I thought you may find Mum's story of interest.

My mother grew up on BlueBell Hill in the 1930's and 40's. She told me that her class was taken on a nature walk as a school outing to Kits Coty Barrow, an ancient Barrow in the South East of England, the day went well and they were busy collecting plants when one *little girl started screaming and pointing to the woods surrounding the field.*

When asked the young girl explained she had seen a Giant Ape Man in the trees and it was watching the girls from the Wood, Of course the teachers got the girls together and walked them back to school promptly. The girl who had seen the creature was very badly shaken and didn't attend school for a week or more.

Kits Coty or The Countless Stones, and also known as Little Kit's Coty House, are the name of the remains of a Neolithic chambered long barrow on Blue Bell Hill near Aylesford in the English county of Kent. The Accounts seem to run in a line, with Kits Coty making the central place? A route as old as time maybe? A landmark that has never changed? Or a place sacred to the Forest Folk in a way it was once sacred to us too?

I did do a little digging into the "school outing" and realised this was around the time many school children across the UK were doing "their bit" for the war, kids from schools across the UK picked hedgerow foods to supplement the rationing and for use as medicines and poultices. This became one of the ways we kept the hospitals here and on the front line in supply of much needed medicines and supplies. Without these children many of whom picked, planted and sorted through materials for anything that could be salvaged, repaired or recycled.

Blue Bell Hill Gorilla 1990's - Blue Bell Hill, in Kent, is infamous for its' ghostly hitchhiker but this area is also a cryptozoology hotspot - an ostrich was seen by a driver during the 1990s near the haunted hill, but what is of most interest to the BBR is that a large hairy beast, thought by the witness to be a gorilla, was seen here. This coincides with the other sightings in the area including that by a group of five Territorial Army members, who shouted and threw stones at the Bigfoot as it ran away.

The so-called 'beast' of Blue Bell Hill has existed in one form or another since the 1500s when a mysterious creature was spotted near Boxley and Burnham. On August 5th 2009 a sheep was killed not far from Blue Bell Hill at a farm which had never, in 40 years, suffered a sheep loss. In the area two piles of fresh excrement were discovered next to the contents of the sheep gut (digested grass) and a few yards away eaten, and cleanly rasped remains of a sheep.

There is another sighting in nearby Chatham made by a young girl with her partner who saw the Apeman appear then run off into the bushes.

Another Witness from the Area was named Maureen Bond had a sighting when she was eighteen. She was with her boyfriend in a rural area when the unspeakable happened to her. It was late at night, in some local woodland near Sherwood Avenue. They were sitting there, chatting as normal couples do. Maureen's boyfriend decided to light a fire. As he was doing so, Maureen became aware that something was watching them. She looked up and just a few feet from them were two glowing eyes. As Maureen looked more closely, she saw that the eyes belonged to a large, tall bipedal creature that was covered head to toe in hair.

It stood a couple of feet above her height, so she estimated the being to be in the seven foot region. She watched the creature and was so full of fear she didn't dare alert her boyfriend to it. She then watched, transfixed, as the hairy creature stepped back into the foliage, concealing itself and blending in with the undergrowth.

Despite it disappearing from view, Maureen knew it was still there, watching them, keeping itself hidden by the bushes. She decided not to tell her boyfriend in fear that he may pursue the thing. So she quietly told him she wanted to leave and never gave a reason. Maureen Bond never spoke of what she saw that night for around thirty years, but she never forgot it. She would constantly question herself and what she saw, believing that she may have seen a devil that fateful night.

Two Upright Impossible Sasquatches. Salisbury, 2018 - Witness Report: W. B: *"I have been looking for somewhere I could report a strange incident that happened not too far from Stonehenge. Myself and my Mother saw something that we just can not explain, "It" was quite far away so I didn't get a close look at the faces or anything, but you could tell "they" were not ordinary people and I'm used to seeing cows and farm animals from far away, because there's animals everywhere in Salisbury so I know we were not seeing "something" you would normally see in the fields, as you drive around in the area you get used to seeing animals or wildlife in the fields, but these were not Cows or Sheep, these "figures" stood out as odd to us, there were two really big "figures" in a faraway field that were standing upright and striding along moving quite fast together, one was light brown in colour the other one was darker, they were moving at a fast pace away from us. We both were so shocked and we kept asking each other if we both definitely saw that.*

At the time I was in the car with my Mum and we were driving back from a visit and I just wanted to stop and get out to have a cigarette and Mum decided to come out with me to stretch her legs and get some air. We were just standing there looking out into the countryside and talking when we saw these two huge "figures" walk out in front of the faraway bushes, if "they" hadn't moved we would never have seen them. They walked from behind the bush and were heading it looked like to the next clump of trees. It felt like "they" were in our line of sight for a good minute or so before "they" moved behind another bush in the field and we couldn't see "them" again after they reached the tree cover, we looked for a while but "they" didn't come back this way? I know what people will say, but they were much bigger than any Cow I have ever seen, let alone a Human. Even from that distance you could see this, and they were walking along at a fast pace, definitely standing upright on two legs, it was just crazy. How can we have seen this is Salisbury?

It was in the afternoon probably 3 or 4 o'clock so the light was good, it hadn't gone dark yet, and it must've been towards the end or middle of February 2018. I've never really been into anything like this, but since I saw what I saw that day I have been trying to find something that would match with what we saw. I just can't explain it, I really want to find out more to be honest. It looked like two "Ape Man" type things, Sasquatch it said on your page, I am not sure what you would call them? But the Sasquatch picture you showed me seemed pretty close to what I saw that day, but not perfect, whatever the were, they seemed more Ape than Human. But that's Impossible. Has anyone else seen anything like this in the area?

Image chosen online by the witness

*We were able to see them for quite a while, I didn't even think of
my phone let alone feel compelled to take any pictures, it wasn't
till after that I thought about that. Why didn't I take a video or a
picture? Which is strange because you would've thought if you saw
something like that, you would immediately want to capture it?
But I just didn't feel like that at all. We just watched them as they
walked, waited a few minutes and got in the car and drove home,
we did keep asking each other "did we really see that" "what were
they" "how could we have seen them. And I'm still wondering that
now".*

Grovely Woods Figure Sighted, 2013 - Witness Report: *"Recently, I
was out riding in Grovely Woods Salisbury, Wiltshire. It was just*

about getting dark, dusk. I was on the horse, and my mum was walking along beside me. About fifty meters ahead of us, there was a very tall, large dark figure, I thought too big to be a person, around perhaps two and a half to three meters tall (though we were relatively far away, like I said, around fifty meters, perhaps a bit less)so I am not entirely sure. But when this creature moved, it moved with speed that was incredibly inhuman like, and moved with a sort of loping stride.

When we were at the spot where I'd seen it run off, I noticed that there was no way a human could have escaped that fast, especially through the trees, since it was quite thick there, unfortunately I did not have time to investigate further, since my mum was a little freaked out and wanted to get away from the area, she had told me earlier on in the ride that she had found half a deer (she said it had been 'ripped to shreds) a few days ago, though it was gone when we were at where she said it was. Would a Bigfoot go for something like a deer? The strange thing is, my horse didn't spook, which is strange, since he is generally quite a nervous animal, could this still have been a Bigfoot if my horse didn't react?

Historic reference to wildman near Salisbury - According to the Historical records a wild man who lived in the woods near Salisbury was shot at when he attacked and tried to kidnap a local farmer's wife in 1877. The creature escaped into the dense woodland and was never seen again.

A15 Hibaldstow 8ft Black Figure Moving Off Into The Reeds. June 2018 - Witness Report. B. L: *"I would like to report a Sighting that happened only yesterday 18/6/18. It was between 1.30pm and 2pm myself and my partner were travelling on the A15 heading* towards Lincoln. There's a layby on the road which is roughly a mile or so from the Hibaldstow turn off. And as we were driving we saw an upright moving figure as we were moving along the road. We saw him about 20 foot past the layby. He was upright on two legs, all black in colour and heading away from the road, he was moving through the reed grasses and on into the bushes where we lost sight of him.

I realise it was broad daylight and there was other traffic on the road, so this should not have happened. It wasn't a dark lonely road at night or in the middle of a vast forest, which is how I've been trying to debunk it to myself, but nevertheless I cant talk myself out of what I saw yesterday. It might seem impossible to some but I am certain of what I saw and so is my partner.

I asked the witness to describe what she saw before we chatted so I did not influence her in any way which is something I do with all the people that contact me.

I say 'him' because his energy was male, at the risk of sounding like a crazy person, I see aura and feel energies amongst other things. His energy continued to intrude in my thoughts for the rest of the day, he knew someone had seen him and he was worried. As for a description he was around 8-9 ft feet tall, and a dead black colour all over. One other thing to note. I have a dashcam in the car so I checked the footage in the hopes we had caught him walking away, and there's a 4hr gap. My dashcam records anything out of the ordinary, ie: heavier than normal braking and even when the engines off and stationary the sensor picks up anything close to the vehicle, randomly recording at 5 min intervals. The last recording was at 12.03 just before we set off for the A15 and then nothing until I used the car again around 4pm that night".

He Was Just Watching me, Aug 2017 - Witness Report. S: "*I would like to report an experience that happened to me just last month, I was unsure about coming forward, and to be honest I still am, I was in Brackagh which borders a road and is near human habitation in Co Armagh, I was out as I like to walk and I was exploring an old stomping ground of many years from my youth. Back then the area was different, as this area is now a nature reserve and is used by dog walkers now on a loop walk trail, you can leave the trails and paths but I doubt anybody does. There are seven peat rompers and I walked three or four of them at least that day, so I'd been out for quite some time.*

As I walked the loop that was farthest from the road, I was walking close to the edge of an adjoining field and when I passed a certain spot I heard the unusual cry of an animal. It wasn't something I could identify, but it sounded in distress, I walked very quietly by the way so I don't think I made any noise on approaching that area, or spooked anything? I stood and watched, listening to see if I could see where this sound was coming from or its source. I could pinpoint the area but not the source. I kept looking around trying to see what "It" was but i couldn't identify anything, and as I walked on my way I was still looking.

I did notice a lot of the trees and they had been drilled and a PVC capsule inserted. This I presumed was to kill the tree and roots? Why I don't know as I dug one out with a knife to examine it. These capsules were in lots of the trees around me as I passed by, there were trees with capsules everywhere?

Anyway I walked up a long straight part of the walk and without warning instinct told me I was being watched, I wasn't scared and was at ease but I knew something was watching me walk by. I turned around and saw a large black figure just standing there watching me, back at where I had stopped at a junction on the path to listen to an animal in distress, but could not see. I looked and the figure stood still and was watching me. This was not a dog walker and my car was the only one in the car park when I left and no one followed me that I do know. This figure was jet black and 6-7 ft tall. It didn't do anything, it just stood watching me up the trail, I looked at him and he just looked back.

As nothing happened and I was not a close threat I decided to put some space between me and the figure in the trees, and as I had moved off I went off track exploring, as I broke through vegetation and areas not walked before I saw some flat areas where something large had bedded down or sat? Strangely I was not afraid but more inquisitive to know more. I did keep checking behind me but saw nothing more. I have seen a few areas where a large animal bedded down like a deer up and around mountains regularly. But these were much larger than the deer beds.

At this point I should say no large animals wander here that I know of and there are no deer. I am telling you this as it happened a few weeks ago. I will post a few pics here from along my route, it wasn't an easy place to navigate and I would have gotten lost where I was in the trees, ferns, brambles and peat bog only for my gps when I went off track. The arrow cursor is where the black figure stood as I was up at the top right looking back down the tree lined track".

Whilst chatting with the witness I asked him how he felt that day before and after seeing the figure? You asked me how I felt that day?

"Well I was walking alone as I have done for years as I enjoy the quiet and natural sounds of nature. Not to sound corny but I was at one with nature and in a very content and happy state of mind. Happy to see my boyhood surroundings yet a happiness tinged with sadness also to see the trees drilled with poison, at the same time as I felt concerned for the area and the current environment in which I walked, seeing the trees damaged and knowing there are lots of changes I could do nothing about. I was feeling lots of emotions to be honest."

"After listening to the animal sound and seeing the PVC capsules I moved on and that's when I felt I was being watched. I was not alarmed or frightened, it was more a state of wonder, as I thought 'why was I being watched and by what? Whatever he was, he was calm, just standing looking up the long peat rompers track. I just thought if my time is up it's up, as I would be no match for the large figure I had seen. It wasn't a human or a dog walker or anything like that, the figure stood out as large and broad and dark in colour. I hope this gives a better insight to my thoughts and feelings that day".

Would it be wrong to say that two minds were walking the nature reserves grounds that day, two minds, worlds apart, with perhaps the same thoughts milling through them, a place enjoyed in youth for its beauty and bounty, revisited in maturity only to find so many changes, some good some bad, but changes all the same, sadly only one has the option of getting in the car and returning to the life he chose for himself, the other? Well who knows?

The Halewood Growl 1983 - Witness Report. J. W: *"Hi there, I'm not sure what this was but here's a possible encounter that happened to myself and some friends when we were children. At the time this happened I was around 11yr old and this happened around 1983/4*

I live in Liverpool UK and grew up in a place called Halewood. There is a fairly large woodland that is intersected by a disused rail line. As far back as I can recall the railway has been out of use so we played there a lot as kids. The woods were a creepy place but lots of us would regularly frequent them, climbing trees or riding our bikes, just doing normal kid stuff, making a racket most day. In some parts of the wood the trees grew closely together and were very thick, making it hard to manoeuvre through them, or even enter into them in some places.

We were looking for flint shards to make spears. Yes, Stig of the dump was on TV.

The railway was a place that had lots of flint. We ended up in what I believe to be a clearing amongst Giant Hogweed. it was very odd, though we didn't get the normal burns that you can get from the sap? We were looking on the ground for suitable shards of stone we could nap easily and just concentrating hard eyes locked on the ground and as we were talking, we suddenly heard an awful growl. Deep, a roughened human-like Growl. It didn't matter where we looked. We were completely surrounded by the dense vegetation and we couldn't make anything or anyone out.

It could have been a person I guess? I don't think it was though and it did stand out as really weird? But it was such a strange sound. We ran as fast as we could, we felt at the time like we were running for our lives. I think I just broke through the greenery and down the hill to the open fields and kept on running".

The Creature by the Stream. Southway Woods - Witness Report.
L.T: *"Hello Deborah, I noticed your account of the two creatures at Salisbury who crossed the field in front of a mother and her daughter and I wanted to share something I remember from A long time ago now when I lived In this the South West. I have never known where to share this before or if anyone other than the people involved would find it of interest.*

At the time I was friends with a Lady who was a medium and very sensitive and she and I would visit each other most days for a cup of tea and a chat. She had a young son and he was of an age where he would go out to play with his friends in the woods and fields as most kids did back then after school or in the holidays. They were safe and happy and came home when they were hungry and tired from a good day of adventure. There are lots of woods, streams, fields and open areas for the kids to play around here.

One day I was at my friends house and her son came home with a really strange story to tell, he explained that he was out with his friend playing in the woods close to the small stream down in South Wray wood when he and his friend saw a very strange out of place "creature" It was just after school and they used the short cut through in the woods to walk home when they saw this strange looking "creature" down by the stream, after watching it for a while he came back home quite excited and in a tumble of words explained what he had seen, my friend believed him straight away as he wasn't the kind of child to make things up.

He went on to explain to us in detail what had happened and what the "creature" looked like, he said "It looked like an ape creature" or something he said. It was dark in colour and hairy all over and was crouched by the side of the stream with it's profile to them, it looked like it was drinking from the stream or cupping something in "Its" hand and bringing the hand up to "Its"face.

We talked about this among the adults that were there and we decided to visit the next day as a group to see if we could see the strange creature he had talked about, there was myself, my friend and my Mum. We headed of to Southway woods, my friend went in first and my mum and I went into the woods behind her, there was a very strange feeling in there, a really heavy atmosphere and you could feel something following along in the bushes us as we walked around in there, there was this strange heavy like sound that sounded like foot falls on leaves that we heard echo through the woods. As if something unseen was following us around not worrying if we heard him.

The atmosphere was very strange. I haven't been back there since then to be honest, and I have moved away now. I just put all this down to my friend being an energy worker so I was surprised to see your Salisbury account and realised we could have been experiencing the same kind of creature?

I have had many strange things happen to me and my family in the past, also my late husband experienced some strange things over the years. Im open minded and im sensitive myself so when I saw your page I decided I'd share with you what happened to my friends son. I have noticed some strange stick structures in Decoy Wood in the past.

Not too far away is this very strange account that may just be of interest to some of you".

What Happens at Wistman's Wood, 2014 - Witness Report: *"Wistman's woods on Dartmoor is a very nice place scenic and wild. Many years ago I learned that Dartmoor was originally covered in miniature oaks, which led me to research the area itself and any folklore associated with this area of the UK. As an avid fan of the unknown I started looking and researching and visiting as often as I could, on many camping trips there as a young one I used to find strange structures made from rocks and wood eg : a design like a mounding grave, lean to's and also trees bent in to form an X shape. I have also been and looked around the caves in and around Wistman's wood but I did not stay in them for very long as it felt like I was being watched when I was in them.*

Later in life I started to think about these things that happened when I was young and I read reports on forums and webpages about wild men living on the moorland (Bigfoot?) Many people think of me and others that research this subject and the people who have had encounters as raving mad, as a child and teenager I have had many dealings with strange going on and the paranormal on Dartmoor, things I can not explain away easily, being watched and the feeling of something being near, Dartmoor is a very wild place and could hold more than big cats that people see up on the moor, you never know what or who is out there".

The wood is also said to be the kennels where the diabolical 'Wisht Hounds' are kept. These are a pack of fearful hellhounds who hunt across the moors at night in search of lost souls and unwary travelers. It is said that they are huge black dogs with blood red eyes, huge yellow fangs and an insatiable hunger for human flesh and souls. Strange ghostly howls and screams are also reported by visitors to the moor.

The Lustleigh Cleave Cavemen - A witness confided that she had been walking alone at dusk one night near the Neolithic earthworks at the top of Lustleigh Cleave on the extreme eastern side of Dartmoor when she had seen a family of cavemen, either naked and covered in hair or wrapped in the shaggy pelts of some wild animals, shambling around the stone circle at the top of the Cleave.

Boggarts Hole Clough, Stones Thrown, 2003 - Witness Report. James Whittaker: *"Before I moved to Doncaster a number of years ago, I was living in an area in Manchester called Blackley. This area has some strange local legends of vampires and boggarts and hairy ape men. I didn't know that back then of course but I have studied Cryptozoology for a number of years now due to this incident and I realise now that Boggarts Hole Clough is close to some of the ape man sightings around Manchester and is close to the Werewolf and Big Stinker accounts from Yorkshire. Me and my family would often go for country walks embracing the beautiful woodlands and surrounding.*

Back in 2003 we decided to go for an evening walk in the nearby area of Boggart Hole Clough, an area with an amazing size to it with lots of wildlife. There is a stocked pond and a number of streams and brooks,but that was only a part of it as the area is really large and would take a while to walk around it all so we usually visited the pond area when we got there. We arrived at the location at around 9pm, myself, my mum and an ex partner of hers. As we started to walk along the path, we could hear the birds and the common sounds you would expect, leaves rustling and crunching underfoot.

Everything was fine at first but as we made another step along the path the atmosphere changed in a second, we all felt it at once and without saying anything we had all stopped dead in our tracks. The sudden feeling of being watched swamped us but due to the darkness in Boggart Hole Clough we couldn't see a thing apart from the trees and shadow that were pretty much in front of us and to all sides of us other than the path.

We just stood there for what was probably a split second but it felt like an eternity and the next thing we knew a small stone landed centimeters in front of us. It didn't fall down from above but came out of the trees. As my Mum's ex began to proceed to walk towards the area it was thrown from another stone landed, and then a third.

During this time we felt constantly being watched by somebody or something. It was by the third the stone came flying that we knew it was time to go, we turned and we left the area and I don't think we ever went back.

The Keswick Stone Thrower 1990's - Witness Report. C.C: "It was about 31 years ago now when this happened. My husband and I went to Keswick in the Lake District. For a short break We decided one lovely day to go walking through some dense remote woods not far from where we were staying but far enough that we wouldn't be constantly meeting with other people along the trek. We found a track that was suitable for me and followed it in. We were just walking along there enjoying the trees when everything changed.

We all of a sudden came to a clearing. We stood commenting on what a surprise to find such a clearing in the middle of woods this dense. We carried on talking then for some reason we both froze and all the hairs stood up on our arms. We didn't speak at the time *but both of us felt the same. All of a sudden the birds stopped singing and everything went still and quiet. We sort of froze to the spot, stood completely still and neither of us dared to say a word.*

It was at this point we had stones thrown at us from the trees, they were landing near us but not quite hitting us. Then I said to my husband lets just walk back and act and talk as normal as if it never happened. We did walk back but all the while we knew we were being followed and whoever was following us they were really, really close. At the time I thought it was the panther or one of the large cats we have that the government deny but then with the stone throwing I thought it was a raving mad man as cats can't throw stones. Anyway, it felt as if we were escorted to the edge of the wood and we knew it."

Ashridge Woods Growls and Objects Thrown July 2015 - Witness Report: *"I was walking around Ashridge Woods in Hertfordshire like I always do when some odd things happened which I have ruled out all possibilities of it being something that you would normally find in the woods. I was taking my usual route and I had not passed any else along the path when from within the trees I had something small thrown at me like a fir cone. It didn't come from above but from the trees and then I heard a low growling noise. I couldn't place the animal that made it and I couldn't see anything and I just felt like something was watching me. I couldn't shake the feeling something has "Its" eyes on me, I felt I was being watched before down here and I have seen shadows which to be fair with the way my eyes are im not worried about as my eyesight is not the best it has happened a number of times now and I try to* *brush it off but the last two times I saw "It" it really kinda scared me.*

There was a tree in the pathway which seemed too have been placed (no tyre tracks though that I could find and it was to big to be rolled over there) I also looked around for stumps in the ground as there was no where it would seem this tree had come from I looked over the whole area but I didn't think it could be anything to worry about rather something to keep an eye on but then today it has completely gone again no tyre tracks or dragging marks seen. There was no sign of the tree at all"?

Bardney, Lincs. Shadowed, Watched and Figures in the Trees?
Summer 2017 - Witness Reports. E.H: *"I would like some advice on an incident that happened earlier in the Summer to me and my wife when we were out in one of the areas we like to walk. It did not feel like we were alone that day. It was around 9.15 in the evening and it was a lovely summer's night and I'm not a hundred percent sure, but I think it was late July or early August. We are lucky where we live that we have quite a lot of small woodlands in the area if you google Southrey, Lincolnshire you will see. My wife and I had been for a walk with the dog and we had just parked the car just off the road that heads to Bardney.*

You can walk just inside the woods until you come to the farmland on the opposite side. We followed the perimeter of the woods for a while until we came to a small opening then we both took the path to the left and followed along until it turned right, where it was slightly more overgrown and hard to get into I would imagine, that led almost in a straight line back to the Car. As we started back we were just walking along chatting when we heard something to our left inside the tree line where the rough area is. It was a sound that caught our attention, the sound of "something large walking along with us" "It" seemed to be walking and keeping up with us, keeping pace with us - when we stopped "It" stopped. "It" sounded as if "It" was not that far in, so I started taking photos. I'm a keen photographer and I love wildlife so my camera is always with me. We carried on and by now my wife, who I must say is a non believer, had picked the dog up and started walking back to the car at a pace. I on the other hand wanted to know what "It" was so I walked slowly up the path and I know there was definitely "something" in there. Although I couldn't see "It" I know it wasn't a Deer. A Deer would not make a racket like that or draw attention to itself in this way. This "thing" didn't care if we could hear it.

I took dozens of photos and looked through them on my computer when I got home. I deleted some of them as I went along, but kept the few I wasn't sure about. This was the only one I found that seemed to show something, and this was about halfway back to the car.

6/11/17

I went back to the place we originally went to and retraced my steps back to the area I took the photographs in, but I couldn't find the exact spot as it had changed so much in the last few weeks. I need to spend more time there and get to know the area really well if i'm going to solve this puzzle. I couldn't make anything out as it looked so different in the Autumn. A lot of shrubs and stuff had died down and trying to match the trees was a nightmare. Even with two devices, I couldn't replicate the exact shot - I suppose I will just have to keep returning as the seasons change. I will keep you updated on any finds or further strange experiences".

Like many of the Lime woods, Southrey Wood is a site of Special Scientific Interest (SSI) because of the richness of the plant and animal life found there. It is particularly renowned for it's butterflies.

There is an exceptional concentration of wildlife in the ancient woodlands, and a number of species can be found here that otherwise occur in Britain only much further south or west. The farmland surrounding the woods retains ancient streams, hedges and ditches, supporting scarce species of wildlife. Like the woods, the network of habitats were fragmented, limiting the opportunities for wildlife to expand their range and colonise new areas.

It is advisable to return soon to take a comparison shot of any anomaly found in a photograph or video. Check things like the height of a branch or the width of a tree and hold something there for scale. Many a researcher have tried to get back in months later to find that a lot has changed. In a perfect world it would be easy to match light, season and time of day, but try to get the best shots you can. Two phones, a digital camera and phone, or a mixture of your tech items will help you with this. Hold one device with the original shot open, and try to line it up with the second., and take shots of the matched area a number of times with a slight movement between them. Eventually you should be able to see if the anomaly matches with something within the woods and trees.

Interestingly, this area is one mentioned in old folk lore due to the name of the fields there, "In Stainfield church, near Bardney, are to be seen the helmet of one of the Tyrwhitts of Stainfield, with the family crest of a wild man, with a dagger hanging underneath it on the wall."

He believed the legend grew up around the crest and dagger in Stainfield church and dates from somewhere between 1700 and 1850. He then goes on to relate the story of one Francis Tyrwhitt-Drake who was promised all the lands of Stainfield, including its 280 acres of woodland and the land of neighbouring Lissinglea, if he would kill the wild man who had long terrorised the district. As the wild man lay asleep on a bank by a pit, his presence disturbed a peewits' nest and the twittering of the angry birds attracted Drake's attention.

Seizing his chance, Drake ran the wild man through with his sword. Mortally wounded, the monster jumped up streaming with blood and chased Drake for a mile through the fields before he fell dead. According to some versions of the story, the wild man's blood staining the fields gave rise to the name of the hamlet, but in truth Stainfield, mentioned in Domesday, derives its name from the Scandinavian "stony feld (field) and ford". The "Savage Man" or "Woodwose" that forms the supporter of the Tyrwhitt crest is a heraldic symbol representing strength, honour and fertility, it was a popular choice of supporter with baronets in ancient warlike days.

As a matter of interest, the crest can still be seen on the signboard of the 16th century Tyrwhitt Arms public house at Short Ferry, near the neighbouring village of Fiskerton. A further variant of the tale states that The Wild Man was killed not by a bold knight, but by a group of local farmers known as "The Hardy Gang". Having had enough of The Wild Man killing and eating their livestock, they hunted him down and killed him after a fierce combat in a wood between Langton and Stainfield still known as "Hardy Gang wood."

Another informant relates a whimsical version of the wild man's demise: "I always understood that Mr Tyrwhitt poured a barrel of rum in the pond where he knew the wild man drank, and he drank the water and got drunk and that is how they killed him." Further research into the wild man saga led me to a series of letters published in local news papers. In a letter headed "Refuge from the Armada" a reader from Essex offers the theory that the wild man could have been a surviving Spaniard from one of the many ships of the great Armada that was wrecked by storms in the North Sea.

He writes; " The theory is that a survivor of one wreck, evading capture, escaped inland and lived in the woods around Stainfield of strange garb and countenance, speaking a strange tongue and depending on what food he could steal, it is not surprising he terrified the local inhabitants who regarded him as a wild man. Certainly the clothes I saw in Stainfield Church many years ago, a helmet,gloves, and remnants of a leather jerkin, are not inconsistent with such a theory."

The Hairy Man of Cooling Kent sighting 2011 - Witness Account. F.B.M: *"In 2011 My son and his friend were in the fields when they saw a "very large hairy type man"running along some hay reels. In the early hours before morning light they were both out getting set up for the day before setting out to the fields. They both said "the man-like creature saw them too and then "It" took off running at great speed across the hay reels headed for the woods. I don't think they saw "Its" face clearly as they mostly saw the "creature" as it moved off.*

They said "It" was really tall and was all hair covered. They also said this "thing" had some sort of weird hair at the back almost maine like, and "It" seemed to span its head around as if using the hair to hide "It's" face. They said "as soon as "It" saw them looking at"It `` this "thing" used"It's" hair to cover "Its" face It then took off running on two legs and "It" was moving very fast across the top of the hay reels moving with ease and off up toward the woods.

This happened in Cooling Kent, the experience frightened the life out of them both. We are also surrounded by the Thames Marshes that are very vast and go on for miles. We didn't think of Bigfoot to describe this "thing" until I was surfing the net and I asked him about the description of what he saw that day, we pulled up a number of upright hairy creatures up on google and we found numerous bigfoot images, one of them he agreed looked like the "thing" he saw and he won't go up that way anymore".

Jan 2019 is the latest report to come in to me and it came from this very area, a lady out walking her dog saw something moving along the railway embankment trying to stay hidden, it was a really cold frosty day and there was very little cover afforded to the "strange dark hunched figure" that the lady reported, she said she could see it quite clearly.

Isle of Grain Sasquatch Creature Sightings, 2016 - Witness Report. R.H: *"This report came to me through the British Bigfoot Research Group on Facebook and I am still in contact with the gentleman who reported the account to this day.*

Hello Deborah I'm reporting this on behalf of a good friend, a friend of mine who lives in a remote Kent farm house along The Medway on The Isle of Grain. My friend has lived at this property a number of years now and they experienced some very strange goings on at the Farm. At one point they saw what can only be described as "a large sasquatch type creature" which was on her property on a number of occasions.

Described as "a tall hairy upright creature that looks like a cross between a man and an ape" walking upright on two legs. They would see the "creature" on a number of occasions but "he" was always quite far off from us and would avoid people if he saw them coming. There is a caravan (mobile home) standing on the property and this has been rocked and banged upon on a few occasions now when people have been inside or when it's empty you can hear the noise from the house.

I asked my friend to explain what this "creature" looked like and when they described the height they said "the creature itself has been seen leaning over a Ford escort Van, and he wasn't standings straight up but was hunched over and the roof of the van still only came up to its stomach on this thing."

There are very few houses in the area. If you go there and have a look around you can see how it wouldn't be too difficult to get around unseen out there, situated in between Allhallows and the Isle of Grain the area is a wildlife haven and is protected under law. As I say it's quite isolated. There are lots of water sources and a few woods, it gets more wooded if you follow the river not too far away.

It's been seen by our friends up fairly close, and doesn't seem to be put off by their presence. I have been invited out to camp so I'm going to spend time looking around the sightings spots. We live in the area ourselves on a local farm and have seen what looked like a very large print of something laying down as if a large "animal" had made a bed or a nest of some kind in the tall grass? We are local to a river, power lines, disused train tracks and plenty of woods and forests."

East Grinstead Unknown Creature. What Shadowed Me In Those Bushes? - Witness Report. G.R: "I was contacted by a gentleman on youtube who after hearing one of the video accounts that I had shared from a witness on the Medway felt he needed to get in contact with me in the hopes I could shed some light to an experience he had a number of years ago as a young chap, after chatting for a long while and gaining his confidence he kindly shared his encounter with something strange whilst out on his mountain bike when he was younger, as regular readers will know, mountain bikers and the mountain bike trails are a great source for witness accounts. I have also come across many vandalised paths and trails on the national bike route which runs all across the UK. Large logs and boulders placed on the tracks that are far too large to move by hand yet seem to have been placed there anyway with no sign of a machine or tracks? Wires stretched across the track and in some cases small "pig traps" which essentially is a pit holding sharpened sticks covered with debris to impale any unfortunate passer by.

"Well Deb this is the strange encounter I had in the woods late at night on a solo mountain bike ride in the winter. I will try and make sense of what happened but I am not very good at putting things down on paper and this event is not the easiest thing to explain. I am pretty sure this was back in 2011 as I was around 18 when it happened. It was definitely during Winter as the woods were bare of shrub and leaves and the muddy/clay ground was a nightmare to ride on and I remember it being cold. I used to be a very keen Extreme Mountain biker and I would go out with a group of riders and also I would go solo.

My favourite time was the night rides during the winter months at which time I would usually have a lot of fun, but not this particular night. To be totally honest I have never been a real fan of the dark but after this event I never went into the woods at night again and I still refuse to do so now. I was on my todd (alone) in the backwoods of Cobham on a set route that runs along the North Downs directly opposite the town of Rochester which is on the other side of the River Medway in Kent. That night I was making my way home through the woods and I was not seeing or hearing any other people at all. The woods were empty of other riders.

I mean this place was dark even with my 1500 lume light on my helmet. The area itself was still pitch black, blacker than soot! I must have been halfway between Rochester and Snodland but traveling through the woods on top of the downs not the normal road route when everything happened. Along a part of this ride I started to get a creepy feeling, you know when you don't know why? But you are instantly on your guard and you feel all the hairs on your body stand up as if you are being watched from the trees. I was already cold and covered in wet mud and water so I'm really not enjoying myself any more, I am also in the dark on my own crapping it and confused.

So I stop for a break after doing a long climb up the hill, I make myself calm down and catch my breath, but I can't shake the feeling and I am sure I am being watched. I can't shake the feeling. I look all around me and it is pitch black in the tree cover and I can't see anyone or anything. I then realise how quiet it has gone and that unsettles me a lot as I can't even hear your normal countryside noises now, no sounds like foxes screaming or moving around, owls and critters moving through the grass, nothing! The mood felt extremely off and creepy and I decided to just go home.

I still have to carry on riding to get there so I decided I wanted to get out of the woods now and out onto the road as I am not ashamed to say I felt scared. So I decided to exit the woods and head in that direction leaving whatever was watching me behind. But as I kept on I swore I could hear "something" moving off to the left of me about 30 foot away in the trees and brush shadowing me, I didn't dare look in that direction as to be honest I was crapping bricks by this point and I didnt want to see "what" or "who" was keeping pace with me in the woods. But soon I got closer to the country lanes and it all stopped. I couldn't hear "It" following me anymore and I didnt feel on edge and all the anxiety just left me.

That's about all I have got to say about this experience. And up until 2 yrs ago I had never heard or knew creatures like Dogmen and Wildmen existed. We all know about Werewolves and we are told that they are only Hollywood creations made to create a good movie but when I saw your video on the Medway that is where my thoughts went.

It hit me straight away bringing the whole weird and horrible night back to me. Since that night I had never gone into the woods at night walking or riding and for the last 3 yrs I haven't rode mountain bikes at all".

The Howler of Horsleygate Woods, 1989 - Witness Report. G.H: "It was around 1989 that this happened to me. I was around 17 at the time. I went into the woods for a look around as it's all pine trees and thickly wooded. I was about 100 yards into the wood when it all went very quiet, there was nobody around the wood other than me that I could tell. The atmosphere changed and all around me went deathly still, I stood there looking and all around but I couldn't see anything or make anyone out. Then I heard some *whooping like noise and knocking sounds, only for a split second then everything went silent again, just like that, completely quiet. No Birds nor car noise, no animal sounds, just complete silence.*

I didnt see "who" or "what" made the noises, but I could tell I was being watched the whole time that wood is thick and the trees are large so I couldn't make out "anybody" or "anything" around me. I was getting really spooked at this point so I headed down towards the small stream and got down in there thinking if I hid myself I would see who was making the racket but from my position I saw nothing that would explain all this away. I just lay there for ages, Be careful what you wish for springs to mind as I did some knocks and the whoops started again, even louder this time, my cheeks were puckered I was so spooked.

I looked back into the thick woodland and my eyes saw loads of shapes in the sunlight but nothing I could pinpoint. Then Bump, Bump, Crack in the distance, I could not take it anymore and I was off, I went back to my bike as fast as I could and all the way out, I could feel I was being followed. I was so scared I kept turning around to see if I was being followed but I couldn't see anything. As I left the woods I could hear the natural noises return, the Birds and stream noises. It was over and I have never returned to the wood but have passed close to it many times but I have never been tempted to go back there".

The Wood itself is in Peak District National Park an area of outstanding beauty and importance, situated at the southernmost point, the area is mostly uplands, its highest point being kinder scout, it's vast habitats vary from moorlands to marshy bogs to thick woodland.

The witness in this account has researched the bigfoot phenomena both here and world wide because of this event happening to him, as many of the witnesses have myself included. The event is one thing, the constant questions last a lifetime and we can sometimes be our own biggest critics. Forever debunking what "il" wasn't in the search of what "It" was.

I spoke earlier in the book about being "brushed off" as a child and I know it has happened to a number of people who when reporting things to their parents or peers were just dismissed. No matter the subject matter whether UFO or Ghost, Demon or Djinn the witnesses themselves have to work out on their own what happened to them, back in the day UFO witnesses and Paranormal witnesses were laughed at and ridiculed yet now in 2019 it's almost fashionable to have experienced the like, back when these subjects were seen as "weird" or "alternative" they were whispered about in dark rooms and kept hidden. Yet they have now almost become "the norm" many people the world over are happy to now accept these events happen and that ordinary people from all walks of life report them.

My biggest hope is that the subjects mentioned in this book will also be accepted and the witnesses within will feel not only believed but championed for having the courage to be some of the first to speak out on the subject of "hairy unidentifiable creatures or strange unexplainable events. From the accounts I have taken the reports have always happened, people just chose not to share them outloud with anyone for fear of being rebuffed or thought of as "off" and who can blame them, the stories don't fit into any box or can be wished away from your memory. So I feel collecting them and keeping them all in one place so we can share with each new witness as they make contact is very important. Maybe like the old folklore people will still be speaking about these events hundreds of years from now.

North East Accounts, Derbyshire Moorland Beast, Bi-pedal Figures and Snarls. - A fellow researcher and filmmaker Chris Turner, who whilst busy with his new film Elusive a documentary on the British Bigfoot was contacted by a fellow who had some experiences he wanted to pass on. Chris then kindly passed them over to me here at British Bigfoot. The young man in question is making no claims here, he is merely sharing some strange experiences whilst out wild camping that had happened to him and others over the years.

Witness Statement in Their own words:

"My first experience with what has become known as the North East Derbyshire Moorland Beast was in the August of 1984. I was bivouac camping with my cousin at a place called Blackamoor, Totley just outside Sheffield. I was about 14 and I was visiting family during the school holidays. We had set up the tents and camp, and it had been a fun day and as evening drew in we called it a night. I got into the tent at around 11 pm and we both decided to try to get some sleep.

It felt like no sooner had we settled down to sleep that we heard what I can only describe as "the deep growl" of what we'd supposed must be a large apex predator. That may sound far fetched, but that's what the growl sounded like at the time. It was not something we had heard before or could identify and I am used to the normal noises up there even as a boy. We both shook with fear instantly & struggled not to wet ourselves it really was that bad. We lay breathless in silence as we listened to heavy footfalls moving through the heather around us. Something large was moving around us and it sounded like it was walking like we do upright on two legs.

We wouldn't look outside while this was happening and after a while we raised a bit of courage and gripping our knives we managed to get up out of the poncho shelter. A thick moorland mist had settled and we could barely see each other in it, let alone anything else, we kept searching the fog as we hurriedly packed, whilst all the time praying for all we could muster, strange how you suddenly find the need for God when you feel you are in danger. We went quickly as we could back down to the street lights at Totley and home".

The Niner's Quarry "Thing" Knottingley, 1989 - Witness Report. C.A: *"This event happened to me back in 89 and was probably either late summer or early autumn as there were plenty of leaves on the trees and I don't remember it being cold that night. Myself and my friend Lee had decided to pay a visit to a creepy quarry late at night that was close to us. Niners Quarry as it is known locally has a reputation for being haunted and being quite young at the time it was a sort of dare to go late at night and see how long you could last before running out. As I say Niners is a local nickname for the quarry, the actual name is Park Balk Quarry just south east of Knottingley.*

We arrived at the Broomhill side main entrance about 12 midnight and as we walked down along the main path we noticed a small fire burning to our left, there didn't seem to be anyone about attending the fire so we kept on walking and went all the way through to a wooded area, which is sadly no longer there, but back then it was near the south west boundary of the Quarry.

The night was still and fairly mild as I remember with just a light breeze. It was quiet and we appeared to be alone. We decided to walk back along the main path and as we did so we once again arrived at the fire which was dying down. We sat for a second wondering what to do and not really wanting to go home yet, we talked about it for a minute and then we decided to walk up onto the ridge on the northern boundary, this can be seen on google maps and appears like some steps going down from west to east.

We got up onto the high point of the ridge, and surveyed the quarry below which was about 30-40 ft down to the floor, we could see most of the Quarry from this vantage point. I was about to turn to Lee who was standing beside me and ask if he had seen anything when a sudden noise from below caught our attention. The quarry floor was limestone so anything down there and moving would make a noise that stood out quite well, the noise we heard was loose limestone being disturbed as something 'a figure' moved very quickly from about level with us to our extreme left, "It" had been hiding behind a large slab of rock, out of our viewpoint.

Whatever "It" was it was mesmerising to watch this "thing" For the brief few seconds we saw "It" in view the speed was incredible like an olympic sprinter but yet the noise "It" made was minimal.

No features could be made out, "It" was almost like a shadow, just a "dark figure" moving quickly across the rock and shale. "It" disappeared to our left, our view obscured by the ridge itself and couldn't be heard anymore. We stood in silence and slowly turned to face each other, Lee was mouthing the word 'what' but didn't get any further as he turned to face where the "thing" had disappeared the noise started again, loose limestone being disturbed by movement, "It" was getting louder and closer, 'It' We realised at this point "It" was using the cover of the rock face to approach us unseen.

It happened very quickly, suddenly the noise stopped directly beneath us. Silence! We turned to face each other once more, not looking puzzled anymore but now concerned, scared. We didn't have any time to react. I will never forget the next sound we heard. Below us was a grassy steep sloping bank which gave way to a sheer limestone rock face about 30 ft high. What we could hear was the sound of loose rocks falling to the ground, whatever "It" was "It" was climbing up! As we realised this together the sound had already stopped and I remember we were both staring down at the point where the rock face joined the grassy bank. A "dark figure" was there moving stealthily towards us through the grass!!.

In an instant it was like a spell had been broken, we turned and just jumped about 8 ft to the field below. We both hit the ground hard and for a second, a horrible second I thought my legs would buckle and I would be left alone, but somehow I managed to stay up and then I was off running. I looked round whilst still in the field but nothing was behind us. We ran most of the way through Broomhill estate. What the hell was it?

We went back the next day during daylight and stared in disbelief at what "It" had climbed up in about 3 seconds. It would have taken me ages. The rock face is a good 30 ft high! We even brought a rope and tried to recreate what "It" had done. It took us minutes rather than seconds. And then there was the way "It" moved very fast and stealthy. In that respect it was more like an animal.

Days had gone past since our first encounter. We discussed at great length what "It" could have been. Normally you would have a rational explanation but we just couldn't explain it. Now come on, just how do you climb up a sheer vertical rock face of 30 ft in 3 seconds or less in the dark? We decided to go back in the dark. Not late this time, and we had something for protection. My gran, who is sadly no longer with us,used to live on Broomhill estate, Knottingley. About half a mile north of Niners. So it was a good place to meet, Lee and myself got ready at her house. We were going prepared this time.

I had a BSA meteor air rifle on which I had 'under slung' a powerful 3d cell torch. Not exactly a 12 gauge but it felt good to have it as we climbed over my grans back garden wall and headed for Niners once again. The night was still and quiet as we walked across the fields.

We arrived at the quarry about 9.30 pm. This time mounting the ridge at the east corner overlooking a pond below us. We made our way back along the ridge occasionally dropping back into the field due to brambles blocking our path. We didn't go down into the quarry this time, after the last time we just observed from the relative safety of the ridge. Nothing could be seen on the quarry floor and there was no noise either. We cautiously approached the area where we had jumped down and scanned the scene below us. I had a rifle and torch ready but I had not used the torch much until now. I reached for the on button and as I did so Lee patted me hard on the shoulder 'there' he was saying in a loud whisper.

I followed his pointing and could see "something" behind one of the large slabs of limestone, I could see part of "It" it's hard to describe in words but "It" looked like the same "thing" a dark figure, with no features. It kind of had a mesmerising effect to watch. It was terrifying but at the same time fascinating.

As I stared at the "figure" I could see "It" appeared to be watching us and "It's" upper body was heaving like "It" was out of breath and gasping for air as if "It" had been running hard. Again as if a spell was 'broken' I turned the torch on, the beam was very bright and lit up the area well so as I swung the rifle around towards the figure I remember thinking 'right, this is it, were going to see what "It" is' As the beam drew near to the figure the torch suddenly cut out, I frantically pressed the on off button to no avail, I banged the torch with my palm this didn't work either, it was just dead and I had specially put new batteries in for this night.

Our fear was reaching boiling point, the "figure" was still there and could 'attack' at any moment. I couldn't fire at "something" if I didn't know what it was so I aimed at the rock "It" was behind. I indicated to Lee to run as soon as I fired. I didn't hesitate. I just fired a warning shot and I didn't wait for any consequences. I heard the pellet hit the rock and that was it, we were off across the field sprinting to my gran's house. After a 100 or so yards we glanced around behind us whilst fast walking to catch our breath but couldnt see anything. Upon getting back to safety in the house I double checked the torch, it came on! I flicked the switch off/on several times, it worked every time. What caused the malfunction? And was that "figure" the same one that we had originally seen? This time it hadn't tried to approach us, was this because it was not something strange but because "It" knew we had a weapon? We would encounter this "thing" again.

In the coming weeks we continued to visit the quarry both during the day and at night. We would only see the "figure" at night and only fleetingly. Once whilst being chased by a large gang we made our escape via a small path that led past Niners and out into the fields, we had just got onto this path adjacent to The Broomhill estate and as I ran I glanced to my right, the entrance to Niners could be seen through the dark about 100 yds away, I noticed a "dark figure" stood perfectly still near the entrance on the main path, "It" just looked odd in a sort of hunched over position with no features to be seen as "It" was just black, I only saw "It" for a few seconds, but that wouldn't be the last time.

We had become quite obsessed with seeing this figure and told one of our friends Nick who decided to come with us one night. So all together off we went across the fields from my Grans house, it was about a 10-15 min walk to the quarry, the night was still and clear as the time was around 9 pm. We decided this time we'd go in on the main entrance just like we did on the first night. I'll explain here that if you're looking on google maps it is not the Womersley rd entrance, this is where the lorries used to go in, its a wide path across the field from Broomhill estate.

We walked down this path and as we got closer the atmosphere just sort of changed, it became more expectant, you knew something was going to happen, but you just didn't know what! Suddenly there was a commotion of barking dogs coming from in front and to our right, they were in the garden of the house next to the main path, on the right of the path there is the boundary fence and a house with a large plot of land.

The dogs belonged to this house. Occasionally they would bark at passers by but as we approached the entrance we realised that they weren't barking at us, they had gathered next to the fence where it bordered the quarry and they were barking eagerly at something hidden to us, whatever "It" was "It" was in the bushes next to the fence. The dogs really were going mad!.

We went past the commotion and carefully walked a little way into the quarry. The dogs now were muffled a little by the shrubs and bushes. We were confused and curious as to what they were barking at and so we just stopped and stared towards the bushes.

What happened next was like a dream, it was very surreal.

I remember hearing first the bushes moving and then seeing branches and even whole shrubs shaking and bending over, snapping etc. But not being able to see what was doing it. "Something" was moving through the undergrowth rapidly towards us. With the amount of noise this "thing" was making you could tell "It" was big at least as big as a large man. There was a barbed wire fence that bordered the bushes and separated that part of the quarry from the main path. As we all stood staring in a kind of fear and fascination induced trance, this fence was hit by something, like someone had just run straight into it! You could hear the wire creaking and cracking under the strain, then, an instant later it just stopped.

I had a horrible feeling, I heard and 'felt' "something" big and heavy dash past me very close. I didn't see anything. But I felt the ground at my feet 'shake' as "It" went past. I spun around quickly to see nothing! There was nobody. How could that be? We all stood in stunned silence. Slowly 'coming to' from the experience.

Nick had been a little way off and had not felt the vibration and heard the "thing" run past but had seen the bushes moving and the fence. Lee had been standing close by and had felt the ground shake just like me. I don't think we ran but walked quickly and quietly back to Broomhill, I remember we didn't want to go back across the fields.

We had no rational explanation for the event. To this day we still discuss it, between ourselves

Although I have lost contact with Nick, I do still see Lee regularly and he helped me with this report as my memory isn't what it used to be. There is a striking similarity between this 'thing' and my other report of the one in Paull. A dark figure, predator like, very agile and seemingly possessing a supernatural ability.

But, there is a distance of around 45 miles between Knottingley and Paull and of course this sighting took place 13 years earlier, could the sightings possibly be connected? Both times I/we had the strong feeling "It" was 'playing' with us, "It" could have done something to harm us at any time, we were at "It's" mercy but "It" chose not to do anything.....is this proof of some kind of empathy"?

The Broomfield Dog like Beast, 1990/94 - Witness
Statement: C. Shaw - *"I grew up in the countryside close to Essex, UK. We lived in a very rural area surrounded by thick woods and fields back then and there was a small farm down a single track road.*

My first encounter with this "thing" that I can only describe as a "beast" was in our garden at about 11.30 pm when I was about 13/14. My step Dad had just driven back from the pub and was in the kitchen making toast and I went down to get a drink of water. The back garden flood light was switched off as it was very blinding when it came on. My step Dad noticed something moving about in the garden as he was looking out of the window. He questioned what he was seeing so I took a look and as we tried to work out what "It" was but we could not make it out clearly so he switched the flood light on.

In the light we can see now alright, as plain as day this "thing" was on all fours drinking water from our pond. "It" was huge. "It" was black and very wide and very muscular. "It" turned and looked towards the house. I am assuming "It" couldn't see us from as we were shielded by the blinding light. I've never seen anything like "It" before. "Its" face was just like a dog but "It" looked much more fierce than any domestic dog and " It's" features were very strong and defined. This "Creature" was covered in thick black hair from head to toe.

My step Dad and I just stood there in shock. "It" moved away from the pond and stood up on "It's" back legs and leapt over the end tall garden hedge. This hedge was about 10 ft tall and "It" had no trouble clearing it. Then "It" was gone. My step dad turned off the light and told me to get to bed. The next morning he told me that we were never to discuss what we had seen again. Whenever I tried to mention the event and what we saw he just denied it all as if it never happened. But that was not the only time I think I came very close to "It."

Another time I was walking my friend home across the fields past the farm's old barn. There was a large broken hole in the side of the barn and we had to walk close to it as we went right past it to get down the track. It was around lunchtime so we were walking in broad daylight. As we got closer to the barn we both noticed this "animal" edged inside of the barn looking out of the hole at us. "It" moved and I knew I'd seen "It" before. We both questioned what "It" was or what "It" could be and we both decided to back off slowly and return the way we had walked. As we did this "It" moved further backwards into the barn I think it did this to remain hidden? We walked back to my house very quickly and I never went down there again on my own that I can remember.

We had a few neighbours in the area who all said that they had heard "weird howling" noises at night. But they were quickly convinced it was just foxes. I grew up in the countryside and I know what foxes sound like and these howlings were not the noises of any fox.

There was one report sent to the police about an unusual animal in the area after something huge ran out in front of a dog walker into *the woods. The dogs refused to walk near to where the "animal" was and sat whimpering, then "It" shot out across the field into the woods. The police got a casting of some prints but then it all went hush and never to be mentioned again? So this is my personal experience and I am thankful that I no longer live in Essex".*

As you can see from the encounters shared in this book, there are a number of strange impossible creatures being seen by children and adults here in the UK dating back to the early 1940's. In my next book we will hear from Adult witnesses to these creatures, and many of the Bi Pedal Wolf reports, commonly called Dogmen. Canine Creatures, that can move upright on two legs, or down on all fours. They have Canine Teeth and Pointed ears. Some cultures call them The Dog Headed Men, Shucks, Wulvers and Bargyst.

People Who Witnessed Dog Men, Werewolves, Wulvers and Shucks. Available now on Amazon.

Deborah Hatswell is a Writer, Blogger, Podcaster and Owner of BBR Investigations, an organisation made up of volunteer Investigators worldwide. Deborah has taken or researched over 1400 personal witness reports. All of which can be accessed freely on the sightings map link listed below. Our Investigators are from very different Genres, we have Paranormal researchers, Cryptozoologists, UFOlogists, Ley Line researchers and many more varied skill sets and strengths. You can join our Investigation team and community group for free. No skills or experience necessary and all abilities and ages are welcome.

If you have a case you would like us to investigate or need help researching please get in touch and we will do our best to help you. We can also feature your book, podcast, website, forum, social media, youtube, online magazine for free in our monthly news email.

To contact Deborah you can use any of the sites listed below.

CONTACT EMAIL - debbiehatswell@gmail.com

MAP OF UK SIGHTING REPORTS - Deborah Hatswell's Cryptid Creatures - Beings - Impossible Events Map.©

YOUTUBE - Deborah Hatswell #BBR ©

MEWE: Deborah Hatswell

REDDIT - Bigfoot Dogman Reports

SPREAKER - Deborah Hatswell. Cryptid Creatures and Unexplained Events ©

PODBEAN - Deborah Hatswell. Cryptid Creatures and Unexplained Events

APPLE PODCASTS - Deborah Hatswell. Cryptid Creatures and Unexplained Events

SPOTIFY - Deborah Hatswell. Cryptid Creatures and Unexplained Events

Made in United States
Troutdale, OR
09/12/2024

22766816R00105